THE LAST BLUESMAN

This multi-layered, multi-faceted story is utterly captivating, and in Morris Jones the author has created the most rounded, well-written character that I've encountered.

— RICHARD WALL, AUTHOR OF *FAT MAN BLUES*

The blues is a strange *beast*. Unpredictable; blindsiding. Ran Walker's *The Last Bluesman* stitches blues with a literary style that is smart, accessible, and unexpected. A collection that resonates like the songs of Blind Willie Johnson, Son House, Albert King, Stevie Ray Vaughan and others. Serious, humorous, sexual, intelligent, and descriptive, *The Last Bluesman* is what makes blues good and novels great.

— VAN G. GARRETT, AUTHOR OF *HOG* AND *WATER BODIES*

The characters become so familiar, their conflicts so realistic, and their dilemmas and dreams so tangible, that as a reader you will feel as though you were in the Mississippi Delta along with them.

— SABIN PRENTIS, AUTHOR OF *BETTER LEFT UNSAID* AND *COMPARED TO WHAT*

The Last Bluesman touches deep in the soul. The words jump off the page, and I feel like I'm right there with the characters of the story. And the Blues...it's ever so present and honest!

— LAMONT JACK PEARLEY, TALKING BOUT
THE BLUES PODCAST AND BLOG, NYC

The Last Bluesman is a Southern tale ripe with lust, regret, death. It epitomizes the blues. Read with a stiff drink in hand.

— JEWEL BUSH, AUTHOR AND FOUNDER
OF MELANATED WRITERS COLLECTIVE
(NEW ORLEANS, LA)

THE LAST BLUESMAN

RAN WALKER

This book was originally published as *Mojo's Guitar: A Novel* by Cool Empire Press.

No part of this book may be reproduced in any form or by any electronic or mechanical means, including information storage and retrieval systems, without written permission from the author, except for the use of brief quotations in a book review.

ISBN: 9781020001246 (Paperback)

ISBN: 9781020001284 (Ebook)

Library of Congress Control Number: 2020915800

Second Edition

10 9 8 7 6 5 4 3

45 Alternate Press, LLC
Hampton, VA 23666

CONTENTS

AUTHOR'S NOTE

When I originally published this book as *Mojo's Guitar* back in 2012, I never thought it would be the kind of novel that would make it around the world. This novel resulted in my forming new friendships "across the pond" and was even translated into French by Philippe Loubat-Delranc and published by Éditions Autrement under the title *Il était une fois Morris Jones*. Following the second edition of the book's French publication, I began to look at the original English language version again with fresh eyes.

The book was first titled *The Last Bluesman* and was published as a novella, before I wrote two other novellas that ultimately merged into a single novel. The 2012 version of myself thought *Mojo's Guitar* would be a good title for this novel. The 2020 version of myself, however, feels the original title was perfect all along.

What follows is the original manuscript, with a few slight changes. If you are reading this for the first time, I hope you enjoy it. If you are reading it again, all I can say is thank you for finding value in this story.

Ran Walker, August 2020

PREFACE

Why I Decided to Write a Blues Novel

This book has been a long time in the making. I came up with
the idea for it nearly four years ago, and when I told my father
about it, he immediately took a shine to it, being the quin-
tessential blues connoisseur that he is.

As I composed each draft, my father shared stories, music,
and articles with me. Having grown up in the Oak Grove
community of Biggersville, Mississippi, he has an undeniable
emotional connection to the music, and his enthusiasm is conta-
gious. It definitely found its way onto the pages of this novel.

After a while, I started working on other projects, but he
refused to let the book take a backseat. "How is the blues book
coming?" he'd ask. I would respond by telling him that I was
working on something more "commercial" and would come back
to it later. Even when *B-Sides and Remixes* was released, he would
tell people about that novel, while hinting that he couldn't wait
for the "blues book" to come out.

So umpteen drafts later, I stared at the manuscript,
wondering if it should see the light of day. This time it was my

wife who picked up the baton from my father. "Trust yourself," she would say. "You can do it." While those words might seem like generic motivation to some people, my wife actually saw my elation, anguish, confusion, and desperation on this project first-hand. So her encouragement has been quite a buoy.

In retrospect, it seems a given that I would have written a blues novel, given that I am originally from West Point, Mississippi, the hometown of Howlin' Wolf, one of the greatest bluesmen of all-time. I grew up around the blues in a way different from many people. It wasn't just music; it was the way people communicated. You could taste it in the food, feel it in the hearty handshakes and hugs, and hear it in voices of people whose wisdom far exceeded my own.

I am pleased to finally see *The Last Bluesman* in print, building upon its earlier existence as a novella. It is my hope not just that you enjoy this novel, but that my fellow Mississippians will feel I have done justice to the subject.

For Dad

PART I
THE BLUESMAN

CHAPTER 1

Coltrane Washington looked up from a short story he was reading when he heard a light rap on the door. He was more than halfway through his office hours at Bondurant Hall, so it didn't surprise him when he saw a young woman standing in the doorway.

"Could you please sign my book?" she asked.

"Sure."

He figured her to be at least twenty by the way she wore her reddish flowered sundress, a matching flower in her shoulder-length hair. The dress complemented her golden complexion in such a way that he found it difficult not to stare.

"I loved your book," she said, approaching the desk and extending a copy of *The Wine of Goddesses* to him.

"Thanks."

"I would've taken your workshop, but I already had eighteen credits this semester. Gotta graduate on time." She laughed lightly, her voice high like a cartoon character. "Are you teaching anything next semester?"

"No. Just the one for this semester."

"Damn," she said, and for a moment he couldn't tell if she was genuinely disappointed or just attempting to flatter him.

"I'll be giving the occasional talk and doing a reading or two in the spring, but that's about it," he offered.

The young woman placed her index finger against the edge of his desk and swirled it playfully back and forth in a loop as she waited, her dark brown eyes set on him.

Coltrane lowered his head and gripped the pen lying next to the stack of stories he had just started grading. "What name should I make this out to?"

"Melissa. Melissa Morgan."

As he began to write, he noticed, out the corner of his eye, her walking over by his bookshelf, admiring the framed photos along its edges.

"Are you married?"

He finished signing the book and closed it. "No, I'm not."

Since he'd arrived, he'd gotten that question more than a few times. He figured people were drawn to him because he was one of the few single African-American males in the English department—and then there was the book, the novel that had helped him to win the writer-in-residence fellowship that was allowing him to be hosted at the University of Mississippi for the year.

Melissa ran her fingers along each of the frames. "You know all of these people?"

"Most of them."

"I wouldn't even know how to act around them," she said, turning back toward him. "*You're* the first famous person I've ever met."

He smiled. "I'm not famous."

"Yes, you are. You're a published author."

"Well, thanks," Coltrane said, handing the book back to her. He wanted to tell her that being published wasn't all it was cracked up to be and that he'd be living off of teaching positions and fellowships for the next few years, if he was even that lucky.

The actual book sales were definitely nothing to write home about, but that was always the dilemma when choosing to write literary fiction over commercial fiction: critical acclaim or money. Only a handful of authors could do them both, and Coltrane knew that he wasn't one of them.

She took the book and immediately opened it to read what he had written. When she finished, she smiled.

"So, like, what do you do when you're not teaching?" she asked, shifting her weight so that her hip appeared even curvier in her sundress.

"Read, write—and grade papers," he said, lifting a stack of short stories from his desk for emphasis.

"I know it doesn't seem like there's a lot to do around here, but you'd be surprised."

"Maybe."

"If you wanted, I could give you a list of things to do. Maybe I could just show you around sometime."

The offer was definitely tempting, but he knew he would have to let it pass. Although he wasn't technically a member of the faculty, he didn't want to do anything that would cause the committee to regret its selection. He could only imagine how embarrassing it would look if he got caught up in a situation with a student.

"I'm fine, but I appreciate your offer."

Coltrane picked up the pen again and grabbed one of the stories from the stack on his desk. Now, more than ever, he needed a distraction.

"Mr. Washington," she said, causing him to look up at her. "When is your next book coming out?"

"Still working on it, but I'll keep you posted."

As she sauntered out of the office, giving him one last good look at what he was passing on, he smiled to himself and shook his head.

~

The Wine of Goddesses was both a gift and a curse. After laboring through hundreds of rejection letters and getting a few short stories accepted by small literary journals that most readers didn't even know existed, he focused himself enough to send out the novel he had been honing for three years. It went out to seven different competitions and another eight small literary publishers. None of the literary agents he had queried showed any interest either.

It had taken nearly a year to hear back from the few presses that he did hear back from, and he was ready to resign himself to the fact that he might just need to start over with a new novel when he heard back from a small New York operation called Holbrook Publishing House in the East Village, just off Broadway.

They wanted to publish the book, they told him, but they wouldn't be able to provide an advance beyond a thousand dollars. His royalty wouldn't be much better than that of a larger commercial publisher, and he could expect to actually pocket around eighty cents for the sale of each trade paperback original that was sold. At the time he signed the contract, he didn't know the first thing about e-books or why the company didn't produce them, yet required that he sign over those rights, nor did he understand how limited the distribution would be for his book. The marketing was so microscopic that he could only compare it to a single person trying to feed a stadium of people with a Halloween-size mini-bag of M&Ms.

Something good had come from it, though, besides the slight critical acclaim the book had received: he had won the yearlong fellowship at Ole Miss in Oxford, Mississippi. Up until that point, he had assumed he would have to continue his job as a teaching assistant at an alternative school in Silver Springs, Maryland. While the fellowship wouldn't make him wealthy by any means, it did mean that he could at least live the year as a self-sustained author.

As he pushed the last of the short stories he had been grading to the side, he looked out the window of Bondurant Hall. William Faulkner had once lived roughly a mile away, and with Square Books in downtown Oxford just a few blocks over, Coltrane thought he would have had more than enough inspiration to begin work on his next novel, but that hadn't been the case. Since he set foot on the campus, his creativity had all but disappeared. It seemed as though he had shifted into promoting *The Wine of Goddesses* and found it difficult to write much more than a page on anything else that he started.

From his office window, Coltrane could see students moving about the campus, some lying beneath the giant sleepy oaks, others riding bicycles, holding hands, or just reading on the steps of one of the other buildings. Somewhere in the distance he could hear the sound of the marching band practicing. The lush green grass was trimmed neatly and eased gently against the snaking sidewalk. In the middle of it all, he noticed Melissa, the young woman in the reddish flowered sundress, moving along the sidewalk in front of his building. He could see her hips swaying sweetly beneath her dress, and he wondered if spending a little time with her might be the thing that could spark his creativity again. He forced himself to look away.

Inhaling deeply, he turned back to face the papers on his desk. The stack of pages from his students' stories left him with a bittersweet pang. While he was proud of their work, he envied how freely their imaginations worked. These kids were years from the kind of writer's block he was now facing. He knew he would have to work harder. He refused to allow himself to blow this year of creative solitude. There would have to be life after Oxford, and for that to happen, he knew he would have to write another book.

CHAPTER 2

S cott Ericsson was the last person Coltrane expected to hear from. They had met only once before at an industry event in New York over a year ago. Coltrane could scarcely remember giving his number to Scott. He did, however, remember talking to him at length about whether Phonte Coleman was a better rapper or singer (after all, there were few people with whom he could have the Little Brother/Foreign Exchange discussion). If his memory served him correctly, Scott worked for a music magazine or something like that.

"I hear you're down there in Mississippi now," Scott said.

"Yeah, I'm at Ole Miss as a writer-in-residence. How is everything in The City?"

"Can't complain. Hectic as usual," Scott said. "Hey, I know you're wondering why I called, so let me just cut to the chase."

"What's on your mind?"

"We're looking for a writer to do a story for one of our upcoming issues, and someone told me that you were already in Mississippi—which is where the guy we need you to interview is."

Coltrane smiled and shook his head, wondering if everyone

outside of Mississippi thought of the state as just a large city. "What kind of piece are you looking for?"

"Something like *Midnight in the Garden of Good and Evil* meets a Ralph Ellison jazz music essay. Can you feel where I'm coming from?"

"Kind of."

"We want to make the story about the individual, but we also are looking for someone to gonzo up the thing a little so that we can get your perspective on meeting the guy, too."

"Who is the guy?" Coltrane asked. He didn't know if there were a lot of famous people in Mississippi. Maybe he was supposed to interview Morgan Freeman or something.

"His name is Morris Jones. He's a blues singer from Oak Bluff. That shouldn't be that far from where you are."

Again with the Mississippi as city ignorance, Coltrane mused.

"Who is he? I've never heard of him."

"I don't think many people have. He cut a record back in '61 that didn't really sell much of anything, but The Crazy Tonies…"

"The English band?"

"Yeah, them. They decided to cover one of his songs in the early 70s, and it became a hit in the U.K."

"Like Eric Clapton did with Robert Johnson's old stuff."

"Exactly. So the editors at *Midnight Jukebox* decided that we should do an issue devoted to these forgotten bluesmen who inspired so many of the English rock and roll bands. I have writers assigned to Charlie Patton, Howlin' Wolf, Muddy Waters, John Lee Hooker, Robert Johnson, and a few others, but when I found out that Morris Jones—they call him Mojo— was actually still living in the Mississippi Delta, I knew we had to send someone out there who could sit down and talk to him."

"Well, I appreciate your keeping me in mind. I don't know much about the blues, though."

"Don't worry about that. We can have an intern send you a

packet of materials that we put together already, along with the contract info—that is if you're interested."

Coltrane paused for a moment to consider the offer. He knew he'd have to give an answer to Scott when he opened his mouth. That was just how it worked with New York City professionals. Scott would have a string of calls to make when he hung up the phone and probably wouldn't have the luxury of waiting a day, especially if the production department was already preparing the layout for the issue. That was one thing Coltrane relished about The South: the luxury of time. It largely moved and swayed with the breeze, giving the illusion of camping out in the nooks of trees, only to move a little more slowly—it seemed—than it did elsewhere in the country. People simply didn't rush; there was plenty of time to get where you were going and to do whatever it was you had to do. In New York, however, the city held a certain speed that seemed to accelerate the importance of nearly every-thing. The natural flow of the city was so much faster paced than everywhere else in the country that tourists could be picked out easily, simply by the way they bottlenecked the sidewalks of Midtown, providing the natural flow of the city with that unin-tended hiccup. So Coltrane would not be on his own schedule, if he accepted the job. He'd be on a New York schedule.

While he could have easily passed on the assignment, he knew he had to take it, if only to be writing for a purpose that resulted directly in publication—and money. Scott had planted the seed by mentioning Ralph Ellison. Coltrane knew that if he were to survive on the literary landscape beyond *The Wine of Goddesses*, he would have to write a number of essays and short stories to keep some sort of presence out there. Of course, a novel would be most ideal though.

Midnight Jukebox was a well-respected magazine with a read-ership of around two hundred and fifty thousand or so. Who knew? Maybe he could eventually publish a collection of essays or get an idea for a new novel. He knew he was getting ahead of himself, but without the luxury of time, in the Southern sense, his mind raced like lightning streaking off a greased hog's back.

The only thing he had to deal with was canceling his only class that week. He'd just give out an assignment that he could take up next week. His students would understand. After all, his being published was a good thing for everyone.

"Okay. I'm interested."

"Good!"

Scott laid out the terms of payment, as well as the article length, and agreed to ship a package via Fed Ex that would arrive the following morning.

When he hung up the phone, Coltrane stepped outside of his townhouse and into the downtown square that sat only a few blocks from campus. He admired the quaint look and feel of Oxford. It reminded him of a Norman Rockwell painting. The courthouse was situated in the center of the town square. It was what he imagined Faulkner's Yoknapatawpha County to be like, from the little bit of Faulkner that he had actually finished. He wasn't sure how far he was from Oak Bluff, but he knew that Oxford was only a short drive from Batesville, which he knew wasn't far from The Delta. He had been curious about the area, but up until Scott called him, he had not made any plans to go there any time soon.

Now he had two reasons to go: a publication credit and a check to match.

CHAPTER 3

Coltrane's first thought on seeing the flat, plain-looking land of The Delta was that it seemed to stretch on forever down Highway 61. There weren't many houses either, just spacious fields of cotton and other crops lining the highway and large flashy billboards for the casinos in Tunica. With all of the empty, uninhabited land, he had a fleeting thought that made him nervous: what if his car broke down and a mob of rowdy rednecks suddenly came along looking to lynch him? How far would he have to walk to get to an exit if his car broke down? He quickly checked his cell phone signal and was relieved when he saw several bars and a fully charged battery.

Off in the distance, he could see large casinos looming over the barren flatlands like palaces. He assumed he was only half an hour from Oak Bluff, but that was before he came to understand that the casinos weren't actually *in* Tunica, but roughly ten miles north of the actual, and much less majestic, town of Tunica.

He glanced at the Fed Ex package on the passenger seat. He had spent the previous day reviewing its contents and down-loading blues music from the Internet. He had learned that there were two general styles of blues music: the kind that most Northerners thought of as traditional blues music (which had its own subset of Delta, Chicago, St. Louis, and Memphis blues, whether acoustic or electric) and the more contemporary type of blues music that sounded like older rhythm and blues, but had lyrics that covered every conceivable blues theme. He was particularly fond of a song called "These Last Two Dollars." He even enjoyed The Crazy Tonies cover of Mojo's song "Love Slaughterhouse," although he couldn't find the original version online. As far as he knew, he was headed to interview one of those legendary bluesmen, the ones most people associated with the blues: the ones who owned old beat-up guitars, wore gold teeth (or had missing ones), drank from liquor bottles filled with homemade hooch that they carried around in their coat pockets, and smoked cigarettes that dangled from their lips like old bicycle kickstands. As this thought crossed Coltrane's mind, he shook his head. If he was going to write a solid, worthwhile story, he had to shake any of the stereotypes people already held. He knew he would have to dig deeper for his article to have any real substance.

Then he felt the butterflies fluttering in his stomach. He wasn't sure why, though. He'd hardly ever been nervous about anything when it came to his writing, but now he wrestled to ignore that growing discomfort. He realized that this story had to be written, but he also realized that he had not written anything in quite some time and prayed that the article would not be a disappointment.

Something deeper was gnawing at him, though, as he prepared to take the exit for Oak Bluff, something he had tried to ignore when he first started doing his research. The hunger had intensified, and deep down, he began to harbor fantasies about starting a new novel once he finished the article. He cautioned himself against getting too excited, but zooming pass the intersection of U.S. 49 and U.S. 61, he realized that if Robert Johnson could, as a matter of legend, create a Faustian bargain at this metaphorical x-spot, then anything was possible.

And that realization both excited and frightened him.

~

THE MOTEL WAS SIMPLE, BUT CLEAN, WHICH WAS ALL Coltrane really cared about. The skinny, pimply redheaded kid behind the desk appeared to be not much older than sixteen. He wore an orange tie and a navy blue blazer so large in the shoulders it made him look like a Shogun warrior.

"If you need anything, just call down to the office," the kid said, sounding like he had a wad of snuff packed in his lower lip.

The sun hung lazily in the western sky, a golden sphere floating in a vast blanket of pinks, oranges, and blues. Coltrane marveled at its beauty for a moment. It had been a while since he had taken the time to notice a sunset, and he found himself standing frozen, staring off into the horizon. Over his shoulder, the moon glowed like a china plate, and stars began to reveal themselves in the haze of transitioning colors.

He would call Mr. Jones in the morning and set up a time to go by and interview him. Take everything a day at a time, he told himself. His article would be due in a week.

He inhaled deeply. He could do this. This was a necessary part of his plan, and he knew that when the rubber hit the road he was indeed a clutch player.

CHAPTER 4

The alarm on Coltrane's cell phone screamed like an ambulance siren in the silence of the room, forcing him out of bed. He stumbled around, heading for the bathroom.

The water pressure in the shower was so weak that he struggled to stay awake. He rubbed the coarse facecloth across his eyes. He wanted to crawl back into bed and sleep for another hour, but he knew that he needed to grab a bite to eat and get started with his day.

He had learned that there was a blues museum downtown, so he would go there first and do a little research. He would need to give Mr. Jones a call and see if the old man would be around that afternoon, and hopefully that was where he would close out the day.

Tossing on a polo shirt, a pair of jeans, and some running shoes, Coltrane grabbed a bagel and a cup of orange juice from the continental breakfast display downstairs and headed for his car. The drive downtown didn't take long, but as he cruised around through the back neighborhoods, he was shocked at how dilapidated the buildings were, especially those that ran along Martin Luther King, Jr. Boulevard. It was difficult to tell which storefronts were open, because each of them looked as if, ironi-cally, it had been bombed out during the riots that erupted from King's assassination in 1968.

He hopped out of his rental car, digital camera in hand. Ignoring the curious autumn heat, he walked down the street, snapping pictures of the different buildings. In the distance, he could hear heavy voices rumbling, voices riddled with dark, percussive animation, as if they were somehow attempting to occupy far more space than their bodies would allow. Before Coltrane realized it, he was standing several yards from five young men who looked at him as if he had picked the wrong place to park his car.

"Look at this nigga," said the tallest one. His violet colored baseball cap sat squarely on his head like Elmer Fudd, and his pants hung below his crotch area, revealing Tasmanian Devil boxers.

"Awe, that nigga green!" another one said, pointing at Coltrane and laughing.

There was a strange kind of irony to the situation, Coltrane noticed. Having lived in Atlanta, New Orleans, and the DC metro area, three areas notorious for crime, he had never been mugged, yet here he was, standing in the streets of Oak Bluff, Mississippi, realizing that none of that really mattered.

As they steadily approached, Coltrane considered a cowardly sprint for the car, but something in him didn't want to let this group of kids get the better of him, Oak Bluff or not.

He gradually worked his way down the street toward the car, but the group of boys moved into the street cutting him off.

"You lost, nigga?" the tall one said.

Coltrane stared coolly at the kids for a moment, accepting the fact that he could knock out at least two of them in a fair fight, if there were such a thing anymore. He glanced around at the buildings that seemed like they would fall down all around him and then looked back at the kids. This was their neighborhood, as raggedy as it appeared, yet in a few years, all of this area might well be gentrified and these kids would have to pull up their pants and work at the neighborhood Starbucks. Even with all of those thoughts coursing through his mind, Coltrane still wasn't about to let those kids whip his ass.

"Before you do anything stupid, let me tell you that I just got back from doing two tours in Afghanistan. I'm trained to kill. You guys might take me, but I'm taking at least three of you with me. You can believe that shit!" he said, flexing his frame a little.

Coltrane had been working out for the past five years, and while he was often confused for a college football player due to his fairly solid build, the only sport he had ever played was tennis. These kids didn't know that though. As far as they were concerned, every piece of bullshit Coltrane had just uttered was the gospel.

The tall one stared him down, waiting for him to flinch, but his pride wouldn't let him.

"A'ight, man. We was just fuckin' wit you anyway."

They walked past him, their voices a low mumble. He imagined they were talking about the ass whipping they would have served him, if they hadn't given him a pass.

Coltrane walked back to his car and exhaled a sigh of relief as he drove back onto the main strip and headed farther downtown.

THE BLUES MUSEUM WAS LOCATED IN WHAT LOOKED LIKE A dead-end alley. It had once been a train station, but through a little creativity and a few grants, it had been converted into a tourist attraction.

Coltrane didn't know what to expect when he walked through the front door. The museum's layout was very simple: framed pictures lining the walls and several instruments encased in glass, resting on display stands. At the back of the room was what appeared to be a replica of the shack Muddy Waters grew up in. The swinging rhythms of acoustic guitars and heavy, soulful voices resonated around the room, and for the first time in his life, Coltrane realized he was surrounded by blues music.

As he scanned the pictures along the wall, he came upon one with the name Morris "Mojo" Jones beneath it. Mojo had a dark complexion and a low salt and pepper haircut, but the angle of the picture revealed the deep grooves in the man's face and the thinning patch of hair across his scalp. His complexion was a few shades darker than Coltrane's, but he looked as if he could've been a distant relative. The old man's short-sleeved shirt and suspenders gave him the look of someone who relished the simpler things in life. Coltrane suddenly felt the urge to talk to him.

Wandering back into the gift shop area, he found a portly red-faced man with a ponytail pulled from the few strands of hair that ran along the sides of his head. The man sat behind the register perusing a magazine. The glass counter in front of him contained all sorts of souvenirs, everything from t-shirts of Tommy Johnson to stone necklaces of Charlie Patton and Muddy Waters.

"Excuse me," Coltrane said.

"Yes. What can I do you for?"

"I was just wondering if you knew anything about of a blues singer named Mojo Jones."

"Ole MoJo? Yeah, I know exactly who you're talking about. We actually have a picture of him in the back there," the man said, pointing to the main room of the museum.

Coltrane nodded. "Yeah, I saw it. I'm writing an article for *Midnight Jukebox*, and I'm in town doing a piece on him."

"*Midnight Jukebox*? Sweet, man, sweet. Well, welcome to The Blues Museum," he said, shaking Coltrane's hand. "My name is Ed Wagner. 'Wag' like a dog, not 'Vog' like the Germans say."

"Nice to meet you, Ed. I'm Coltrane Washington."

Ed laughed, as if Coltrane had just told him the mother of all jokes. "For real? I get it. That's some kind of name."

"Yeah, tell that to his parents," Coltrane responded playfully.

"Well, Mr. Coltrane. I know a lot about the blues--so if you need any quotes or anything, you just come by and holler at me. I'm always here."

Coltrane started to go ahead and interview him right then, but he wanted to build around Mojo's interview and fill in from there. "I will definitely take you up on it."

He glanced around the display case. "I don't see a lot of stuff on Robert Johnson in the museum. I would've expected to see a little more on him, with his popularity and all."

Ed chuckled. "I can definitely tell you're not from around here. Most people think that Robert Johnson *is* the blues. He was definitely good, but most of what people know about the man is all wrong. He got a lot of his skills practicing chords he picked up off of Charlie Patton."

"What about the Devil and the Crossroads?"

"That was Tommy Johnson. They don't even know if Robert made the deal or not."

Coltrane tried to conceal the expression of incredulity burning behind his eyes. He had half-expected this guy to discount the story as mythology, not revamp it. "Well, that will definitely need to be something we get to in our interview."

"No problem, man. I'll be here most of the time during operating hours."

"Thanks again, Ed," Coltrane offered.

Before he left the museum, he went back into the exhibition room and took a long look at Morris "Mojo" Jones's picture. The old man's sallow, wide eyes looked as if they had seen far too much.

Coltrane walked out to his car and called the number Scott had given him. It was time to get started.

CHAPTER 5

According to the directions, Coltrane was a little over three miles from Mojo's home. With all of the streets being only two lanes, he didn't know how long it would take to actually drive that distance, regardless of what the GPS said.

The traffic was sparse, and many of the houses in this rural area were spaced out by what looked like at least a football field's length. Every other house looked as if it had come from some old black and white photograph, something from the days of the Freedom Riders. He had entered another world, where dilapidated buildings were like worn-out piano keys on an old baby grand. The tone was there, but it was strained.

His GPS signaled that there was a turn coming up. Because of the flatness of the land and the lack of trees (or anything else, for that matter), he could see for at least a mile without obstruction.

He continued to creep along until he saw a mailbox reading "Jones." He had never seen a shotgun house before, but looking at Morris Jones's house, he could clearly see how such a house earned that name. The faded mint green structure was narrow and nearly all wood, and it looked much longer than it was wide. The rooms appeared to come consecutively in the house. It didn't seem like there was much of a hallway, just room after room after room. Even more interesting, there was an odd, narrow porch built onto the front of the house, wide enough to hold two small chairs, one on either side of the entrance.

The concrete sidewalk leading from the gravel driveway to the house was worn and cracked, but a footpath had been worn into the grass on both sides, as if visitors preferred walking through the grass to get to the porch steps over just taking the sidewalk. Sensing that he had better take the grass as well, Coltrane walked around the sidewalk.

He knocked on the screen door after seeing no doorbell. Unlocked, it rattled loosely in the doorframe. He rapped against it a few more times.

"Yes," a woman responded, her voice easing through the cracked door.

She couldn't have been more than twenty-five. Her complexion was the same rich brown color as his own, but there was a glow to her appearance, as if the sunlight was kissing her skin. Her hair was pulled back into a bun, and a pair of small, stylish glasses rested atop her nose. She wore a yellow t-shirt and a pair of cut-off denim shorts that emphasized the toned shape of her legs. Her lips, though, those full and succulent lips, appeared to be crafted by God for the specific purpose of kissing someone tenderly between soft-spoken affirmations.

He stared for a moment before formally introducing himself. "Hi, my name is Coltrane Washington, and I'm here to see Mr. Morris Jones."

She smiled. *Lord, she has the sexiest dimples,* he thought.

"Come on in," she said, opening the door wider. She extended her hand. "I'm Erica Townsend."

Her hand was soft, and the thought of being intimate with

her was fleeting, but *strong*. He had not been around a woman who was not connected to Ole Miss in some way, and he smiled, finally free to bask in the glow of a woman's beauty, without reservation.

"Mojo!" she yelled toward the back of the house, releasing his hand. "Mojo, we got company!"

The figure at the back of the house was tall and dark with a thin frame. From where Coltrane stood, he could see the size of the man's hands, and it reminded him of the time he had shaken hands with Jerry Rice. Rice's hands were so large they swallowed his like a giant glove. Now as Morris Jones walked closer, Coltrane noticed not only the man's hands, but his height as well. He had to have been at least 6'5", because Coltrane felt as if he had to strain his neck to look up at him.

"Mr. Jones?"

"Call me Mojo," the old man said, his voice deep and raspy. "You must be the young man who's gon' write my story."

COLTRANE WAS PLEASANTLY SURPRISED THAT THE CHAIRS ON the front porch felt more comfortable than they looked. He sat facing Mojo, his digital micro-recorder in one hand, a pen dangling over a notebook in the other. Erica walked up to the screen door, holding two glasses of water. He quickly stood to hold open the door for her, subtly admiring her appearance. She smiled and handed one glass to him and one to Mojo.

"You don't mind if I ask you a few questions, do you?" Coltrane said, returning his attention to Mojo.

The old man took a long swallow from what looked like a tiny glass in his huge hand, and Coltrane watched his Adam's apple rise and fall, like a lever pulling weights. "You the writer, so ask whatchu need."

"How did you get started as a blues singer?"

"There's a hundred ways I could answer that."

"Okay," Coltrane said, starting again. "When did you first begin performing music?"

"Now see, I can answer that 'un. I was down at the Sheriff's ranch when I was a youngster, working off my debt to society."

"Sheriff's ranch?"

"Yeah. That's where they used to send the boys too young for Parchman. I got it in my head to steal from this general store with a few friends of mine. We ain't get nothing more than a few pieces of candy, but that's the way it was back then. I guess I shoulda been glad that it wasn't no worse than that. A few years later, while we was still at the ranch, they killt that boy Bobo Till. All he say was 'baby' to a white woman and they got him. Ain't nobody could sleep for months after that."

As Coltrane listened, an image of the Emmit Till pictures from *Jet* magazine crossed his mind. He couldn't imagine the kind of effect something like that would have on the kids who were around when it happened. For a moment he watched Mojo look down at his glass, as if the old man was remembering something it seemed he wished he could forget.

"What was it like inside the Sheriff's ranch?"

"They worked you like a old mule."

"Like an old mule?" Coltrane said, scribbling in his notebook.

"You ever heard that joke about Bessie the Mule?"

"Can't say I have."

"Well, there was this man who was driving along in the country, and he done fooled around and got hisself stuck in this ditch on the side of the road. He had to walk 'bout a mile to the nearest house, and when he got there, he asked the old farmer who lived up there if he could help get that car up out the ditch. The old farmer told him he could do that and went out back to get his good ole faithful mule, Bessie. The farmer hooked up Ole

Bessie to the car and yelled out, 'Pull, Buster, pull! Pull, Millie, pull! Pull, Bessie, pull!' When Ole Bessie done heard her name, she pulled like the devil and got that car up out that ditch. That man looked at the old farmer like he was crazy as a loon. He say, 'Old man, why you call out all them names 'fore you done call out Bessie name?' That farmer leaned over and whispered to the man, 'Ole Bessie is blind as a bat. If she knew she was gon' pull yo car by herself, she wasn't gon' pull shit!'"

Coltrane doubled over laughing. "Good one," he said.

"Awe, man. I'm just tellin' it straight. But to answer yo question about that ranch. Man, they worked you like a sharecropper's stepchild. That's the way you paid yo debt back then. And doin' that for a few years was enough to let you know not to fuck up again. I wasn't gonna graduate into no Parchman. Hell, no. There ain't no such thing as easy time up in Parchman."

"So you never went to prison?"

"Not a day. I got my shit straight on the ranch. Picked up the gee-tar there."

"Why the guitar?" Coltrane asked.

"Because I couldn't blow harp worth a rat's ass."

"Harp?"

"Harmonica," Mojo responded. "I just worked with the bottleneck. Back then, them was the only two instruments, 'sides the drums, that could get a fella some pussy."

Coltrane laughed hard and nearly spilled his water again. Behind him, he could hear Erica walking through the house. He suddenly became curious about the relationship between Mojo and the beautiful young woman moving around in the house. He wanted to be tactful though.

"Are you related to Erica?"

"Not really."

"What do you mean?"

"My last ole lady, rest her soul, is Erica mama."

"It's just that you two seem pretty close."

Mojo took another swallow from his glass and continued, "See, I was with her mama, Ruby, up 'til she passed away. Problems with her sugar. We courted for about ten years. Erica was in college part of that time. But when Ruby passed on and then my own health started getting funny, Erica started droppin' in on me. I told her I was a'ight, but she kept on comin'. Now she be over here all the time lookin' after me."

Coltrane nodded, thinking about the fact that he had lost one of his own grandmothers to diabetes complications. "When did Ruby pass?"

"Not even two years back."

"I'm very sorry to hear that."

Mojo nodded and looked away.

Coltrane took a sip of water before picking up his pen again. "Do you have any other family around here?"

"Nope. I'm the lastest of my family, and I ain't even the baby. I had two brothers. My big brother Jerome died when this guy cut him at a party. Bobby, the other one, died from the fever when he was little. Both my parents died 'fore I went to the ranch, so it's been just me for a while."

"Well, now it's you and Erica," Coltrane offered, smiling.

Mojo smiled in return, his teeth too straight and white to be his own. "I can see it in yo eyes, young man. You got a thang for her! It's plain as day. She a good woman, too, and she ain't got no kids neither! Ain't never been married. Shit, she in school over at Delta State working on a masters degree. You oughta talk to her."

Coltrane chuckled, surprised at the comment, and then he wondered whether he was really as transparent as the old man implied. Taking another sip of water, he looked out at the setting sun, its burnt orange and yellow glow spreading out across the horizon, fading into the beginning of night.

"So you don't have any kids?"

Coltrane saw the old man's eyes drop away for a second. "Well, one."

Coltrane sat up. "Son? Daughter?"

"Son, but I don't really know him. His momma went up North and had him before he was born."

"So you two were never married?"

"You ever heard of a shotgun wedding?"

"Not really."

"That's when you get a girl in the family way, and her daddy show up at yo house with a shotgun tellin' you that you gotta marry her to make the child right with the law and such."

Coltrane leaned in closer. "So her father came up to you with a shotgun?"

"Something like that."

"Well, what happened?"

Mojo sighed. "He looked for me, but he ain't never found me. I was floatin' around in them days after the ranch. I ain't have no steady address. But I heard he was lookin' for me, so I split."

"So she went up to Chicago then?"

"Had to. Can't be around here all up in the family way like that."

Coltrane started to furrow his brow but caught himself. He knew if he were going to keep the old man talking, he couldn't be judgmental on what had happened several decades ago. "What happened after she went to Chicago?"

"She had the baby and stayed up there."

"You didn't go up to Chicago?"

Mojo lowered his head. "No."

"So did you ever see your son?"

Mojo kept his head low, not responding.

"Do you know his name?"

Mojo looked toward the road, his lips sealed.

"Beautiful sunset, huh?" Coltrane said, changing the subject.

"Yeah," Mojo said, his eyes turning back to Coltrane. He paused before opening his mouth again. "When you come tomorrow, I'mo play somethin' for you."

"I'd like that very much," Coltrane responded.

He put down his recorder, and the two men stared out at the wide cotton field across the road, the blossoming white bulbs floating atop the brown wiry stems, as they lost themselves in the activity of their thoughts.

CHAPTER 6

The weathered, dirt-colored guitar felt surprisingly light as Coltrane rotated it in the morning sunlight. The strings were as still as corpses, and when he strummed his fingers across them, the guitar moaned in a haunting voice, as if it were coming back to life. He carefully handed it back to Mojo.

"Ole Annie Mae what I call her."

Mojo looked at the guitar as if catching a faint memory, one that would dissolve into oblivion if he were to look away for a single moment. "We been through a lot together."

Coltrane looked away from the guitar and brushed at the sweat on his brow. The sun was already blazing at ten o'clock in the morning, and while he prayed for a breeze to whip across the porch, the air hung still, like an oven. He didn't realize it could get this hot near the end of October.

"So you learned to play the blues on the sheriff's ranch?" Coltrane asked, refocusing himself.

"Yeah, but I had been playin' blues for years 'fore I knew what it really was about. See, playin' yo instrument is just part of it. It just ain't playin' the same chords over and over while a man spill out his heart. It's 'bout pain. And ain't no pain worse than havin' yo heart stomped on by a big-legged woman."

Coltrane could only imagine. "How did you eventually discover what the blues was *really* about?"

Mojo was quiet for a moment, before breaking the silence with his laughter. He ran his fingers across the strings of his guitar. Ole Annie Mae moaned a delicate, familiar response. The intimate exchange between the two of them made Coltrane feel as though he were intruding on a private conversation.

Bringing his wailing strum to an end, Mojo eased his voice into the vibration of the strings, as they decrescendoed into a whisper.

"When did I discover what the blues was really 'bout?" he repeated. "I guess when I realized that my arms was too short to box with God. It's funny. That point when you think you a man ain't really the point when you become a man. Lotta things I wish I could take back. That kinda pain is what the blues is 'bout."

Coltrane wondered if the old man would have done differently by his son, but he knew that was a touchy issue so he left it alone. Instead, he shifted gears.

"Were there any special women in your life?"

The old man's Cheshire grin spread widely across his face. "Every bluesman done had a few women in they time. I once had this woman named Chastity, big ole yella girl, and I tell ya, whoever named her ain't even come close to getting that one right. She was looser than a broke bike chain. You know, the kind of woman that just spread like peanut butter. Thick as a mothafucka, too. She was the kind of woman that put it on you so hard you wanna slap yo mama. I don't know why I wanted to make a honest woman outta her. She was set in her ways. But boy, could she put it down! Ole Mojo used to stand up in it all night. Between Chat and my job, my back went out on me a few times —that's when you know a man be stroking! Back problems and shit. She was too wild though. Couldn't take her anywhere without her smiling at some nigger what came at her. She got pregnant and said it was some of mines—but den she tole that same lie to at least three other niggers. Kid came out looking all yella with grey eyes and shit. Turn out she had a joe 'cross town. White dude. We call dat 'un 'musical chairs,' and that time the white son of gun got assed out."

Coltrane listened as Mojo continue on, rattling through a list of women that seemed rather exhaustive, even by Coltrane's own standards. One would have assumed that the old man would've slowed down with age, but one would have assumed incorrectly. Even Ruby, according to Mojo, had gotten worn down by the ole "magic stick."

"I tell you," he said, catching his breath. "Doc once tole me if I don't use it, I lose it. Didn't want that to happen. Plus, life 'round here wasn't no walk in the park. Sometimes a piece of pussy was all a man had to make him feel like he was somebody."

Even in the bluntness of Mojo's comment, Coltrane could understand, somewhere in the recesses of his brain, where the old man was coming from.

"Did you ever fall in love before Ruby came along?" Coltrane asked.

"Ain't you been listenin'? I fell in love at least a million times."

"I'm sorry. I thought all of those women were just you having some fun, sowing your wild oats."

"Nah, son. I ain't no ho. I just love hard—and often."

"I got you," Coltrane said, laughing along with Mojo.

He stretched out his legs and gazed into the hot afternoon sky. The heat was starting to get a little more bearable—or maybe it was just that he was adjusting. Erica would be coming within the hour, and Mojo had already asked him to stay for dinner and enjoy some of the catfish a neighbor had dropped off earlier that morning.

As he sat there silently with Mojo, he could feel himself melting into the scene around him, as if he now belonged to the earth on which he cast his gaze. At that moment he didn't feel like a visitor or a writer, and strangely, the feeling was liberating.

CHAPTER 7

Even though the house was narrow, the kitchen was arranged as to accommodate an impressive dining room table. It rested against the back wall so that Mojo sat in the center of the table's only accessible side and Coltrane and Erica sat on either end, facing the other. Coltrane found himself unable to look away from her. He didn't want to appear to be staring, but when he thought about what Mojo had said earlier about Erica being single, he couldn't help but size up the situation as they ate.

"So where are you from?" Erica asked.

"The D.C. Metro area."

"Must be nice. Have you met the Obamas yet?"

"Not yet," he responded, smiling. "Actually I've only been there for a few years. Before that, I was in New Orleans up until Katrina. Now I'm in Oxford."

"Oxford—down the road?" Mojo asked.

"Yes, sir. I'm there on a visiting writer fellowship."

"So how did you get to be writing a story for some big time New York magazine?" the old man asked.

"I wrote a book a few years ago, so I guess they thought I could do a decent job with your story."

Erica nodded, and for a moment, Coltrane thought that she might actually be looking at him with some degree of interest.

"So how do you like Oak Bluff?" she asked.

"It's nice. Small. Hot."

Mojo and Erica laughed.

"Guess there's not much to see around here," Erica offered.

"There's enough," Coltrane said, momentarily smiling at her.

Mojo stood up from the table. "Feel like havin' a drink with an ol' man?"

"Sure."

Mojo walked away from the table, and while he shuffled around in one of the dark wooden cabinets in the kitchen, Erica asked, "You ever had any corn liquor?"

"Like moonshine?"

"Something like that," she responded.

"Nah. I've had grain, vodka, tequila, rum—you know, all the hard stuff."

"Well," Mojo said, returning to the table with what looked like a gallon of water. "This here is a little different. Some of this'll put hair on yo chest. This here what we call Bolo. Corn. Catgut. Hooch!"

"What?"

Erica situated glasses in front of each of them. "What he means is that this stuff is so strong that if a possum fell in it by accident and got fished out, any leftover hair would dissolve in the batch."

"Oh damn! I don't know if I need to be drinking anything strong enough to melt hair," Coltrane said, half serious, half joking.

Mojo filled all three glasses a quarter of the way up. "Got anything y'all wanna toast to?"

Erica said, "How about new friends?"

"To new friends," they said, turning their glasses up.

As the moonshine went down Coltrane's throat, it felt as if

someone had launched a blowtorch down into his esophagus. He bent over, coughing and pounding on his chest. "Good lord!" he said, blinking water from his eyes.

"You gotta take it slow at first, young blood," Mojo said laughing.

"It goes down a bit smoother on the second swallow," Erica added.

He took another gulp. Surprised, he swallowed, feeling the liquid slide down his throat almost as easy as water. "It's not bad."

"Welcome to Oak Bluff," Mojo said, tipping his glass toward Coltrane and taking another long swallow.

SHORTLY AFTER DINNER, MOJO EXCUSED HIMSELF TO GO LIE down in the bedroom in the adjacent room, while Coltrane and Erica headed out to the seats on the front porch.

"It's a beautiful night," he said, looking upward. A cyclorama of tiny stars were sprinkled across the darkness and seemed to go on forever. If he had known anything about constellations, he might have tried to impress her with it. Instead, he took in the sight quietly.

"Yeah. I guess I don't look up a lot, but I can see what you mean," Erica responded, swatting at her leg. "You know, you writing this article is a good thing."

"Really?"

"Yeah. Most folks don't know about Mojo. Up until that magazine contacted him about doing a story, he hadn't even talked about music in a while. He'll mess around with his guitar sometimes, but he won't talk about what it was like in the days when he was on the chitlin circuit."

"That's not the only thing he won't talk about," Coltrane said.

"What do you mean?"

"He's pretty hush-hush on anything dealing with his son."

"Oh."

"Know anything about that?"

"A little, but I don't know if it's my place to say anything."

"Of course it's all off the record, you know."

"Still," Erica said. "I just know that the situation that went down was foul all the way around."

"He told me he wouldn't marry his son's mother, so they sent her to Chicago to have the baby."

"Yeah. He definitely did some things that I know he would've probably done differently if he had been more mature."

Coltrane nodded. "Still that doesn't explain the relationship with his son—only the mother."

"Well, I'll just say it like this: sometimes you can't fix a situation, no matter how hard you try."

"So he tried to fix things with his son?"

"I know Mojo likes to joke around, but deep down he's a good man. Ever since I've known him, he's tried to do right by people. I can't see that just applying to people like my mother and me. Know what I'm saying?"

He sensed that she was being intentionally vague in answering his question, but he understood. He hadn't planned on including anything that personal in his article anyway. He needed just enough background so that the *Midnight Jukebox* readers would know that there was a real-life, talented man behind the blues music covered by other artists. With the interview he planned to conduct at The Blues Museum the next day and his remaining interviews with Mojo, he would probably have most of what he needed to put together a rough draft for Scott.

"So what about you?" Coltrane asked. "Mojo said that you were a graduate student at Delta State."

"Yeah. I'm working on my Master of Science degree in Criminal Justice."

"Really? What are you planning on doing with that? I got warrants. I can't be out here talking with the po-po," he joked.

When she smiled, his heartbeat quickened.

"I just want to work in the juvenile justice system. Kids today need to have people in the system who actually give a damn about whether they stay in school and do the right thing."

"Nice. What made you want to go into that field?"

"Mama. All the kids used to come up to her house when they got out of school for the day. She'd let them do their homework there, and when they finished, she would give them candy and snacks and stuff. They loved her. And I believe a lot of those kids stayed in school and went on to do things with their lives because of her."

"I can dig that," Coltrane said.

The combination of her personality and her beauty made him want to ask her out, but he hesitated, unsure if doing such a thing was in his best interest, given that he would soon be leaving.

"So Mr. Washington," she said, with a light lilt in her voice. "You have a pretty interesting name. I already know the who, but please tell me the why. I don't know too many people with a jazz name like yours."

"My father claims that I was conceived while he and my mother were listening to John Coltrane's *A Love Supreme*."

"Wow. That's T.M.I. Too much information!"

"Well, you asked."

"I'm just playing," Erica said, laughing. "So your parents have a pretty sentimental connection with John Coltrane then?"

Coltrane laughed before responding. "You could definitely say that. The funny thing is that *A Love Supreme* is only four songs that clock in at about thirty-three minutes long, so I am kind of secretly hoping that I was conceived during the fourth track, 'Psalm,' if only because I want to believe that my mother didn't get short changed out of the experience."

"Boy, you crazy!"

"But I look like my father, so that must mean that he did something right."

"What do you mean?"

Coltrane smiled. "My father used to say that's how you could tell if a man wore it out in the bedroom: the kid comes out looking just like him."

"Both you and your father are crazy then!"

They both doubled over laughing.

Erica nudged Coltrane playfully. "I read your book."

"For real?"

"Yeah. I was over in Oxford about four months ago at Square Books, and I saw your book sitting on the display table over there. They don't have an urban book section, so when I saw a black woman on the cover, it kind of jumped out at me."

Coltrane nudged her back gently. "I wish you had come to the signing I did over there when I first got to Ole Miss. It would have been nice to meet you."

"Well, you're meeting me now," she said. "I didn't even know about the signing anyway."

"That's cool," Coltrane said. "So what did you think of the book?"

"It was all right," she said, smiling.

He couldn't tell if she was being playful or truthful. "Just all right?"

"It was a nice read. You wrote a book about black women, so you know a sista had to read it."

"What didn't you like about it?"

"I didn't say I didn't like it, but it just left a lot on the table. Like Rose. I wanted to know more about her relationship with her mother, Brenda. I got that Brenda was a loose cannon, but I felt like some of the men in the book might have gotten free passes."

"Like who?"

"The pastor. He should've owned up to the fact that he was

messing with Brenda, but he didn't. You let the pastor's wife square off with her, while the pastor ducked out of the way. I just shook my head and thought, 'this writer must like the idea of two women fighting over a guy.'"

"Well, I didn't mean for it to come across that way. I was trying to show it as being a flaw in the pastor's character, kind of like saying he wasn't worth the effort."

"—and then there was the part where Rose fell in love with a guy who had just ended his engagement."

"They had been on the way out for some time—"

"Still, it just seemed as though everything was kinda rushed. Like if you had taken more time, it would have felt, I don't know, closer to reality."

Coltrane nodded his head silently, casting his gaze out at the stars. His pride stung from her comments. Oddly, she had managed to articulate some of his own concerns about the book. He didn't know why her opinion meant so much to him. It wasn't like she was a critic with *The New York Times Book Review*. Still he felt vulnerable as he stood there next to her.

"But it's a pretty good book. I just thought you'd follow up on the story or write something else. You're a good writer."

"You just didn't like the book."

"I said it wasn't bad. I just know that the best is yet to come. Like that old Grover Washington song."

"Never heard it."

"It's a good one," she said, bumping his arm with her elbow. "Smile. You're too handsome to be so serious!"

He chuckled, feeling himself relax. "Do you have plans for dinner tomorrow?"

"Why? What's up?"

"I was thinking we could get together, have a meal, you know."

Even with her comments washing over him, he realized that he was somehow drawn to her. Her honesty threw him for a loop, but there was something strangely sexy in it. He admired that trait in general, but especially liked it in her. As he waited for her response, he realized that he was even more attracted to her than he had been when he had arrived in Oak Bluff.

"Sure—but I have to warn you," she finally responded.

"About what?"

"When you get to know me, you might want to write a book about me. I have been known to have that effect on men."

"Really," he responded. He smiled at her, and for a brief moment he wanted to kiss her, but he held back, unsure of how she would react. "I'll have to be careful then."

As they looked at the sky, Erica leaned in closer to him, brushing against his shoulder. He enjoyed the sensation of her body so close to his, and for a moment he cherished the comfortable silence between them.

CHAPTER 8

L ying in bed that night, with the air conditioner rattling like the engine of an old pick-up truck on the verge of breaking down, Coltrane tossed and turned. He tried desperately to find sleep in the folds of his bed sheets, but the click and hum of the room played with his thoughts.

The interviews over the last two days had been the first unraveling of his self-identity. Mojo had lived a life full of love, pain, adventure, and art. He was a person who could look you squarely in the face and you would see that he was the genuine article. If Mojo were to write only one novel, it would be because that was the only novel he had in him to write. Coltrane, however, felt the nagging sensation of being unfulfilled--like he had not yet scratched the surface of the writer he could become. He wanted to experience growth in his craft, he wanted to experience more in his life, but, most of all, he wanted to have someone with whom he could share all of these things. He never thought he would have been able to admit that to himself, but being around Erica had made him anxious, and that momentary spotlight on the emptiness in his life had made him all the more curious to know if maybe she could fill it.

He tossed his notebook on the bed and spent the next two hours combing over his notes, his mind occasionally flashing back to Erica's dimpled smile and the promise of their dinner date. In spite of his inexperience with interviewing, he had pulled together a decent collection of notes. Still, he felt that something was missing. It was as if he were on the outside looking in, and when he thought about it, he realized that there were a lot of people who collected blues memorabilia but had never touched the soil of Oak Bluff. To them, blues fit neatly onto a piece of vinyl.

Mojo was the real deal, though. His life's experiences were carved into the lines of flesh in his dark skin, as well as the needle-scratched grooves of his records; they lined his belly and absorbed his pains, allowing them to be channeled through his fingertips into his music. Mojo's blues came from a place that was uncaged and raw, and Coltrane quietly wondered if his writing this article was ultimately doing a disservice to the old man.

He closed his notebook and turned off the lamp by his bed, yielding to one of the most sobering sleeps of his life.

CHAPTER 9

With only an hour's notice, Ed Wagner had pulled out some of his notes and was prepared for Coltrane's interview by ten o'clock the following morning.

After going over some background information about Charlie Patton and McKinley Morganfield (better known as Muddy Waters), Ed had loosened up quite a bit, ready to entertain anything that Coltrane might ask.

"I hope this doesn't sound stupid, but I was wondering what the deal was about The Devil. Is that a metaphor or something? I mean, do people really think that The Devil is walking around The Delta looking to make deals with people?"

"I can't speak for everyone," Ed said. "I suspect that some people do—and who's to say that they ain't right? But most of the bluesmen'll flat out tell you that what they're really talking about is their problems with women."

Coltrane thought about the comment for a second before asking, "But Robert, I mean Tommy Johnson, is supposed to have made a deal with the actual Devil, right? I can't see that deal being about a sour relationship."

Ed smiled. "That's Legba. Scratch. That's what they call him.

That devil is *the* Devil. I'm pretty sure Tommy's talking about him, the same guy that did that deal with the Italian violinist back in the day."

"So it was an actual Faustian deal then?"

"Yeah."

"Do you believe that?"

"I'll tell you this," Ed said, sighing. "I believe that some bluesman wrote about The Devil as a metaphor, but I got the feeling some of them were just telling it straight."

"Are there any stories about Mojo and The Devil or Legba or whoever?"

"Not that I know of. Everyone knows that he learned to play the guitar while he was in juvie."

"Have you ever heard him play—in person, I mean?"

Ed leaned back on his stool, placing his hands on the counter in front of him to steady himself. "This one time. I was at T-Bone's joint out in the county. Oh my god! He was friggin' incredible. Did a little Howlin' Wolf, you know, running his tongue along the edge of the fretboard like so," Ed said, his tongue whipping at the air. "At one point he took the guitar down between his legs, like Tommy Johnson, and he rocked the guitar at the women at the front of the stage, like pow-yow, in yo' face!"

Coltrane chuckled watching Ed pantomime. He couldn't imagine Mojo doing anything sexual with his performance, but then as with many things he was learning, you had to see it to believe it.

"How far back was this?"

"Oh, 'bout, I'd say, fifteen years or so, I'm thinkin'."

"Is T-Bone still around? I'd love to talk to him."

"Naw. T-Bone passed away about three years back. Jealous husband shot him."

Coltrane nodded. "Why did they call him T-Bone?"

"Funny you'd ask. T-Bone was pretty skinny, but to hear him

tell it, he was a walking, talking tripod—a sideways T, if you catch my drift. He and Mojo used to run through some women way back when from what I hear."

Coltrane laughed as he tried to picture T-Bone. "So when you saw Mojo perform, was he touring?"

"Naw, he wasn't on tour. He used to just come through from time to time to play a set or two at T-Bone's. See, from what I could tell, T-Bone used to just pay his musicians with moonshine and a room in the back, if a guy got lucky with a gal in the crowd."

"Well, what do you know about The Crazy Tonies covering his song?"

"Nothing more than the fact that Norm Stone, the lead singer, was a blues fan. I don't know how in the world he managed to get his hands on one of Mojo's records. Back then Mojo had recorded this one album with a record company called Slate Man Records, a tiny label trying to fashion itself off of Chess Records. It was pretty local, but apparently one of the copies got across the pond, and they ended up cutting it."

"So that should've made Mojo a pretty wealthy guy, right?"

"Not in the music business—and especially not back in those days. I would be surprised if he had anything now to show for it. Back in those days, most musicians were happy that anyone even wanted to make a record of their music. I think Howlin' Wolf stands out as one of the few who actually had money. He used to say, 'I'm the only bluesman that drove out of Mississippi' or something like that."

Coltrane underlined the words "The Crazy Tonies" on his notepad. He would have to ask Mojo about that directly. It would seem that something of that magnitude, especially with a Rolling Stones-type of band covering his song, should have made him into a household name, or at the very least a name known beyond the boundaries of Oak Bluff. Sadly, there wasn't anything in Oak Bluff that referenced the old man, other than a very limited reference to him in The Blues Museum. Coltrane could now understand how important it was that he wrote a good article for *Midnight Jukebox.*

He thanked Ed and left. Mojo would have all of the remaining answers.

CHAPTER 10

Mojo was already seated on the porch when Coltrane pulled into the driveway. A small, skinny teenager stood on the porch next to him.

"This here is Jason," Mojo said to Coltrane, while pointing to the kid.

"Hey," Jason said, extending his hand.

"Good to meet you, Jason. I'm Coltrane."

"He a writer. Come to do a story on Ole Mojo."

"Cool!" Jason said.

"We 'bout to get started, so you and me gon' have to finish up later."

"Okay," Jason responded, nodding to the old man.

"Tell Ma Bouf I said 'hello,'" Mojo said as Jason walked toward the road.

"How you doin' this afternoon, Mr. Coltrane?" Mojo said, redirecting his attention.

"Just fine, Mr. Mojo. I see you have Ole Annie Mae out. You teaching lessons?"

"Naw, not really. Jason, he a good kid. You don't find too

many of these youngstas tryin' to learn the blues. I figure I could show him a few things."

Coltrane nodded.

"Hey, you," Erica said sweetly, as she stepped out onto the porch.

Coltrane embraced her. "It's really good to see you."

"You, too," she responded, her dimples dancing. "Well, I'll let you two get back to your interview."

He hated to see her walk back inside the house.

"Tole you she was a catch," Mojo said, unable to conceal his smile.

Lifting his guitar onto his lap, the old man played a few chords, tapping his foot heavily against the elevated wooden porch, causing it to shake slightly, as if a train were crossing the rusty rails of an old bridge.

Coltrane took a seat next to him and looked out at the road. Jason was now completely out of sight. Although the next house was at least a hundred yards over, it was clear that there were only a handful of people sitting outside. The temperature had dropped a little, so it actually felt nice for a change, although Coltrane wished he had brought a long sleeve button-up or something a bit heavier than the polo shirt he was wearing.

Mojo rubbed his hands together, and Coltrane noticed the chalky dryness of the old man's wrists. He looked down at his own hands and noticed that they were drying out, too.

"It's kinda cool out here today, isn't it?" Coltrane offered. "Seems like it's hotter than Hell one day and almost freezing the next."

"Mr. Coltrane, this ain't nothing for Oak Bluff. When the Devil start makin' deals, it get way hotter than what you done felt."

"The Devil?"

"Tommy Johnson ain't the only one making deals with the Devil. I guess, in a way, we all made a deal."

Coltrane quickly clicked on his recorder and leaned in closer. "Did you make a deal with the Devil?" he asked. This was one of the answers he had been hungering for.

"That's not the question you really want me to answer, son. The real question is how many deals *did* I make with the Devil?"

"What? What do you mean? You made more than one deal with the Devil?"

"Most of us did."

"You'll have to pardon my ignorance, but this is all a bit unusual for me, so you'll have to break this thing down. How does one go about making a *deal* with the Devil?"

Mojo paused for a moment, as if reaching for the right words.

"Have you ever did somethin' that you know'd wasn't right for you? Loved on a woman who had another man? Take somethin' that wasn't yours to take?"

Coltrane nodded his head.

Mojo continued, "Some things is just bad luck. It's kinda complicated."

To ease his confusion, Coltrane asked, "Describe the Devil for me."

"She come in different shapes and sizes. Sometimes she big as a house, and sometimes she skinny as a rail, but she got that look. That look get a man every time."

"So you're talking about women? Women are the Devil?"

"Whatchu thank we was sanging 'bout on them records?"

"I had a talk with a guy named Ed over at The Blues Museum, and he said that some bluesmen sang about bad relationships with women being a symbol of the Devil, but he said that some bluesmen were actually singing about Legba or Scratch —a real person," Coltrane said. "Did you make a deal with that devil, too?"

"Now, if'n I did that, you think I'd say somethin' 'bout it?" Mojo asked, looking down at Ole Annie Mae.

"Maybe."

"Well," Mojo said, sighing. "Let me just say this: I s'posed that to write a good blues song, you gotta experience the Devil on some level. See," he said, pointing at his guitar, "Muddy used to talk 'bout his mojo bag. Used to have it to keep the evil spirits away."

"Does the mojo bag have anything to do with your name?"

"My mama name me Morris Jones because she figured as hard as it was for a black man down here in Miss'ippi, I needed have a name that could keep the Devil at bay."

"It doesn't sound like it worked, if the Devil still got to you."

"Mr. Coltrane," Mojo said, raking his fingers slowly across the strings of his guitar, "the Devil get to everybody."

As the sun began to set, they moved into the living room of the house. Erica immediately pulled out an old recording of Mojo's album. The cover featured a faded sepia photograph of a younger Mojo seated on a worn-out wooden chair, legs crossed with his guitar resting gently across his lap.

"Make sure you play those songs for him, Mojo. He's writing a story about your life, and he's gonna need to hear everything you have."

"I know," Mojo responded reluctantly. "I just ain't got to that yet."

"The day ain't getting no shorter," she continued, "and I know Coltrane didn't come down here just to hear you sitting up here telling all those mannish stories that you like to tell."

"I ain't tole him nothing that wasn't true."

Coltrane smiled, rocking up on the back two legs of his wooden chair, careful not to fall.

The small, old record player crackled to life when Erica placed the needle onto the vinyl. A guitar more haunting than anything he had ever heard before filled the room. He couldn't be sure that the sound was the same as Ole Annie Mae's, but it very well could have been. The deep, raspy voice was unmistakably Mojo's, though.

Coltrane listened closely to the music, his ear near the speakers, his eyes on Mojo. He found his foot tapping involuntarily to the beat. Besides the guitar, there was a drum set, what sounded like an upright bass, and a harmonica playing. "Is that you on guitar?"

"Yeah, that's me," Mojo said, nodding to the rhythm of the music. "We cut that record back in the early sixties. Them was funny times though."

"How so?"

"See, what you hearin' right now is Delta blues. By the sixties, folks was listening to Motown and Stax, so not too many folks was buying our music."

"Really? What about your band? Who are the people backing you up on the other instruments?"

Mojo smacked his lips together, as if they had dried out. "Erica, could ya bring me some water please?" he called out over the music

"Sure," she answered.

Mojo looked back at Coltrane. "Let's see. There was Jake Robertson on bass and Jimmy Fielder on drums. Can't say for sure who on harp. Either Joe Brown or Smokey Purnell." He lifted the album cover and stared at it blankly for a moment before handing it over to Coltrane. "Might be on there."

"Joe Brown," Coltrane responded, rotating the sleeve in his hand. "Are any of these guys still making music?"

Mojo looked up for a moment, as though in deep thought. "Jimmy got shot in the eye by a crazy woman he was seeing. I think Joe drank hisself to death. I don't know what in the hell happened to Jake. Last I heard of him, he done gone to Europe to play music. Ain't heard shit from him since."

Erica walked in, bringing two glasses of water with her. She handed one to Mojo and the other to Coltrane.

"Thank you," Coltrane said, smiling at her.

He had been unable to stop thinking about her since the previous night and had been anticipating their dinner. He knew the interview came first, though. Still it was a struggle to steel his thoughts.

Mojo's voice brought him back into the room. "There was one good thing come out of rock and roll for us bluesmen though."

"What's that?"

"Them white boys in England loved us, and because of them, we was able to get a little scratch."

Coltrane nodded. "Have you ever been to England?"

"Nope. But I got a check from there once."

"A check?"

"A young fella liked-ed one of my songs. Said he wanted to play it on his album. I tole him okay. He sent the check. That shit got spent by the end of that week. Ain't heard nothin' about that song since."

"Are you talking about Norm Stone with The Crazy Tonies?"

"I think that name sounds 'bout right."

"And you haven't received anything else from him since he paid you all those years ago?"

"Nope. Kinda funny, too. Used to hear that song from time to time—they version. It was okay, but I knowed that mines was better."

"I think so, too, Mojo," Coltrane responded.

Erica rapped lightly against the doorjamb, stirring Coltrane from his thoughts.

"Mojo, just letting you know that I put some food on the stove for you." She turned to face Coltrane. "And I hope you don't mind, but I felt like cooking today. I picked up some groceries earlier. I'm going to head on back to the house so I can get started."

Coltrane smiled at the thought of her making a home-cooked meal for him. Suddenly, his stomach began to growl, and all he could think about was eating whatever it was that Erica's beautiful hands could prepare. "Sounds good," he offered.

"Well, here's my address," she said, handing him a sheet of paper with nice, bubbly penmanship. "Just come over when you get ready."

Coltrane looked at Mojo, who nodded. "Go on, son," he said. "We're about done here, ain't we?"

"Unless there's something that you wanted to add," Coltrane said. "You know, I'm here for you, to tell *your* story."

"Boy, if you leave that young lady waitin', then you're a bigger knucklehead than I thought," Mojo joked.

Coltrane rose to his feet and looked at Erica. "Well, I guess I'll be trailing you to your house for dinner."

She smiled and extended her hand. Almost as if by instinct, their fingers interlocked.

Swinging his hand back and forth like a playful child, Erica squeezed it and said, "I really hope that you enjoy what I have planned for you."

"I'm sure I will," he responded, as he followed her out of the house.

Erica lived a little over eight miles from Mojo's house in a rather quiet neighborhood on the northern side of the actual town of Oak Bluff. Most of the houses along the street had their lights on over their carports, and with the exception of an elderly man sitting in front of his carport a few houses down, there was no one outside as dusk gave way to night. Coltrane marveled at how different this side of town was from the outskirts of Oak Bluff, where Mojo lived. The area was remarkably middle-class, and he felt a twinge of guilt as he realized that he would have never expected to see a nice neighborhood like this in Oak Bluff, given the crude layout of the downtown area.

"This is a pretty quiet street, isn't it?"

"That's why I like it. Come on in," she said, unlocking the door.

They entered the house through the door under Erica's carport, walking directly into the kitchen area. She hit the lights, and Coltrane immediately noticed the effort that must have gone into decorating her place. The entire color scheme of the kitchen was light blue and gold. A plant with cascading vines trickled over the edges of a gold-painted pot hanging next to the window by the sink.

"Nice place," he said, following her into the den.

"Thank you. I've been here for nearly a year, and every time I think I'm getting the house the way I want it, I change my mind and go for something else. This is the third color scheme that I've done on the kitchen since I moved in," she laughed.

The den was spacious, arranged with a large beige couch and a matching love seat off to the side. Various pieces of artwork adorned the walls, and on the mantles sat pictures of a variety of different people. The only one Coltrane could recognize was Mojo.

In one picture, Mojo was laughing, his long arm wrapped around a heavyset brown skinned woman who had eyes and a smile like Erica's.

"That's my mama," she said, quietly easing up behind him. "I took that picture five years ago at her birthday party."

He nodded, glancing back and forth between Ruby and Mojo. They looked happy, as if they truly understood each other. Coltrane thought about how difficult it must have been for both Erica and Mojo to lose a woman who appeared to have had such a spark.

"Excuse me for a second," Erica said, leaving the room. "Just make yourself comfortable."

Along one of the walls was a large bookcase. He walked over and glanced at the shelves. He realized immediately that Erica had quite a diverse collection, including everything from Sista Souljah's *The Coldest Winter Ever* to Van G. Garrett's poetry collection *Songs in Blue Negritude*. He had half-expected to see old college textbooks mixed in, but her collection gave off the impression of being entirely recreational.

And then he saw it, tucked between two larger books on the third shelf: his own novel, *The Wine of Goddesses*. He usually had a funny feeling from seeing his book in print, mainly because, to him, the book's true nature was that of a stack of paper spat out by his beat-up laser printer.

As he fanned through the book, his eyes caught random sentences that he hardly remembered writing. A bookmark sat at the end of the book, between the last page and the back cover. As he closed it, he wondered briefly how one could feel so close to something, yet so far away.

He placed the book back on the shelf before realizing that Erica had returned and was standing near the door. She had changed from the jeans and button-up blouse she had been wearing earlier into a navy blue baby t-shirt and a pair of short gray gym shorts. If there was a line between function and sexiness, Coltrane sensed that this outfit was walking the line. Everything about her figure was beautiful, from her hair, which was pulled back into a bun, to her nicely pedicured feet.

"I see you found my copy of your book. Would you do me the honor of signing it?"

"No problem," he responded, trying not to stare at her smooth legs. "Sorry it didn't live up to the hype," he joked.

"Come on," Erica said playfully. "I told you it was a'ight."

"I guess I can live with 'a'ight.'"

"On the real, though, one of the things that I did like about your book was that it reminded me of my mother and how we used be with each other."

"Really?"

She smiled. "It made me feel closer to her, you know? It reminded me of a lot of the good times we had together and how hard it was to let her go."

Coltrane didn't know what to say. He hadn't expected that she would have an emotional connection to the book, especially after her remarks from the previous evening. He reached out and placed his hand on her shoulder. She didn't flinch at his touch.

"So yeah. That's what I thought about," she said. "And now I'll have a signed copy."

"You have a pen?"

As she handed him a black ballpoint, she added, "Make sure you put something good in there."

Coltrane smiled as he wrote a brief note about how wonderful she had been during his trip to Oak Bluff and handed it back to her. She read it, smiling, before placing it back onto her shelf. "Thank you."

"No problem at all."

"Guess I should get dinner going. Don't want you to starve to death, especially on my account."

"I'm patient. I can wait."

"A patient man," she said, walking back to the kitchen. "They still make those?"

"I appreciate your cooking dinner. Those pork chops were on point. I see you over there, Miss Iron Chef," Coltrane said, taking his empty plate and glass over to the sink.

"Glad you liked it. There's more, if you're still hungry—or you can take some back with you."

"Thanks."

He turned on the faucet and reached for the dishwashing liquid off to the side.

"You don't have to wash anything. I got it."

"I couldn't do that to you, especially after you cooked such an amazing meal."

"Trust. Those dishes are going in the dishwasher later on."

"You sure? I believe in earning my keep."

"I'll keep that in mind," she responded, winking.

Erica placed her plate and glass in the sink and walked over to the couch in the den. Sitting down, she grabbed the remote control resting on the arm. "Wanna watch some TV?"

"Sure," Coltrane said, sitting down next to her.

He watched as she flipped channels on what appeared to be a fifty-two-inch LED flatscreen. She zoomed through channels as if she were a professional couch potato, registering everything in a glance, her finger never lifting from the remote as she surfed. She came to a dead-on stop when she recognized Julia Roberts and Richard Gere.

"I love *Pretty Woman*," she said. "I hope you don't mind if I leave it here."

"That's cool."

"Hold on for a second," she said, hopping off the couch and turning off the light in the den. She returned and grabbed one of the throw pillows lying next the couch and placed it on Coltrane's lap. She laid her head on the pillow, kicking her feet up on the opposite couch arm. He adjusted himself so that the pillow rested more easily on his leg. This was still a platonic situation, he reminded himself, but it did little to distract him from how sexy Erica looked lying in front of him.

"I'm glad you're here—in Oak Bluff," she said, looking up at him. "You don't know how much it means to Mojo that you came to interview him for the magazine."

Coltrane smiled uneasily, as he attempted to ignore the butterflies flapping wildly in his stomach. They came quickly, and all he could think about was kissing her. He ached at the thought of feeling her lips against his. He had never been this shy when it came to women, but now he felt a newness that gave him pause. The energy in the air felt *different*. And now his actions were different. Glancing at her, he realized that he really liked her and that this wasn't just some conquest or vacation fling. He genuinely wanted to spend more time with her, details be damned. He slowly laid his arm across her stomach so that his hand would no longer be bunched against the couch cushions. She responded by placing her arm on top of his.

They watched the rest of the movie in silence, never changing their positions on the couch, and by the time the movie ended, Coltrane felt as if he had no reason to ever move a muscle again.

~

COLTRANE DIDN'T REALIZE HE'D FALLEN ASLEEP UNTIL THE doorbell rang. He looked down and noticed Erica wasn't there. Glancing around, he found her standing in the foyer, facing the door just off of the kitchen, the one they had entered earlier by the carport. She was absolutely still, as the doorbell rang again and again. Coltrane walked over to her.

"You okay?" he whispered.

Suddenly there was a series of quick, heavy pounds against the door.

"I know you're up in there!" a loud, deep voice barked from the other side of the door. "Erica, I see yo car out here. There better not be no nigga up in there with you! This other car better be yo cousin's or something."

"What the fuck?" Coltane whispered.

"That's Rodney," Erica said, still frozen. "He's *crazy*."

"Well, let's call the police then."

Erica paused before speaking. "He *is* the police."

Coltrane wished he had just gone back to his motel earlier. He hadn't been in a fight since junior high, but as he sized up the situation, he realized he would have to be ready for whatever. He just hoped Rodney wasn't armed. He had gotten lucky with those kids a few days ago, but he wasn't looking to press his luck again.

"He must've been driving past my house and saw your car," she whispered.

Coltrane could see that she didn't know what to do, so he offered, "We didn't do anything. I'm going to just talk to this brotha and see if we can squash this."

"No," she whispered, pulling his arm. "He's crazy!"

"Well, I'm not gonna let this guy beat down your door and

wake up the whole neighborhood." Coltrane pulled his arm from Erica's grasp and walked toward the door.

He opened it and found himself looking directly into the face of a guy who seemed as though he were pulled straight from central casting for an Under Armour commercial.

"Aww, hell no!" Rodney yelled out. "Who the fuck is this nigga?" He pushed his hand into Coltrane's chest so quickly that Coltrane stumbled backward. "This little nigga? Over me?"

Coltrane hardly considered himself a small man, but compared to the muscle-bound mountain that was Rodney, he knew immediately that he was in over his head. Even in fair fight, he would've needed a folding metal chair.

"Rodney, he's my friend! He's in town doing an interview for a magazine!"

"An interview? After midnight? Bitch, you must be crazy!"

At the word "bitch," Coltrane charged him, and Rodney drew back, hitting him so hard across the side of his face that he thought someone had lit a stick of dynamite next to his jaw. He staggered backward as Erica rushed to push Rodney outside the door.

Coltrane watched as they argued under the carport, all the while feeling the screaming ache of his face and what felt like his heartbeat pulsing in his jaw. Rodney was wearing a black t-shirt and a pair of jeans that were so tight they could've been painted on. It might have been comical at any other time.

Stepping out onto the carport, Coltrane considered charging Rodney again, but his mother didn't raise a fool. He enjoyed the sensation of consciousness. And even if his short-term memory failed him, he didn't know if charging an officer in plain clothes was a violation of some law.

"I told you he was just a friend. You always gotta go acting crazy! That's why I can't be with you. I already have too much going on in my life. Don't make me have to get a restraining order on your ass," she said, exasperated.

Coltrane eased closer to Erica, expecting Rodney to flip out, but he didn't. He just stood there staring at her, while Coltrane stood still, his face beginning to swell.

"Why does it have to be like that? I just wanna talk to you. I just wanna make things like they was. Ain't you got some time to talk to me? You ain't been answering my calls. Don't do me like that."

Coltrane couldn't believe how quickly this hulking mass had been reduced to begging in a few seconds. The climate shifted, much in the way it does after a tornado. Just a gigantic brother standing apologetically before a woman nearly half his size. Coltrane couldn't tell what role he played in this situation, so he finally asked. "Erica, are you okay?"

"Yeah, I'm good," she said, shaking her head, clearly aggravated that she had to deal with a situation like this so late at night. She turned to look at Coltrane. "Can I get you some ice or something?"

"I'm all right," he responded in a steady voice.

She nodded and rested her hand on his chest. "Let me talk to Rodney for a minute so I can straighten this out."

Rodney stood silently, not taking his eyes off her. Clearly, there were some unresolved issues between the two of them, and Coltrane figured he had no real business being there. She didn't appear to need him there anyway, and his attempts at chivalry were all but completely embarrassing. Still, he couldn't help thinking how timid she had been before he opened the door and how strong she was now that she was face-to-face with her ex.

Erica walked back into the house with Rodney following. As the door closed, Coltrane considered waiting, but as he replayed the scene that had just unfolded, he knew he would have been a fool to stay.

He glanced at the door for a moment, then got in his car and left.

CHAPTER 12

Coltrane sat in the armchair in the corner of his motel room, nursing his jaw with a bag of ice. The swelling wasn't that bad, and he reminded himself that it could have been much worse: his jaw could have been broken. He could already see the swelling going down, but his ego remained sharply bruised.

His phone had not rung since he returned to the room, and all he could think about were the moments shortly after he had awakened on Erica's couch. Things had moved so quickly, and he hadn't known what he would do when he heard the pounding on the door, but he knew he would have to do something. He still couldn't get over how huge Rodney was. "I must've been stupid as hell to think I could take on that dude," he laughed to himself. The laughter eased some of the embarrassment, but he still needed to hear from Erica, to feel as if everything were all right.

Suddenly Coltrane had a fleeting thought of Erica and Rodney together. They had been a couple before and had probably been intimate in the past. Who was to say that they had not been intimate after he left? He didn't want to believe that, but then again he didn't think that he would be sitting in his motel room at nearly two in the morning changing out a bag of ice to place on his jaw either.

He turned out the lights and lay down on the bed, his phone lying nearby. He closed his eyes, hoping to be awakened by the ringing of his phone with a message that everything was all right, that everything was under control, that he had done the right thing by standing up for her and, ultimately, giving her space to deal with the situation privately.

He slept through the night—dreamless—and the phone never made a sound.

COLTRANE AWOKE THE NEXT MORNING, JAW STILL SORE, BUT the swelling had gone down and now only the dark tint of a bruise remained, evidence of the previous night's scuffle. He checked his phone for messages and felt a second pain, this one in his stomach, as he began to speculate what had happened after he left. For a fleeting moment, Coltrane wondered if he would see Rodney's car if he drove by Erica's house at that exact moment.

The clock read eight o'clock, so he hopped in the shower, dressed, and headed downstairs to grab a bite from the barren continental breakfast display. As he loaded a danish onto his plate, Coltrane thought for the first time about what he would do. He had nearly everything that he needed for his article, so the only reason he could think of to stay around was Erica. After last night, however, he was unsure if that was even an intelligent thing to consider anymore. He hoped that he would hear from her before the day was out, but all the same, he knew that he could no longer justify sticking around Oak Bluff. The week was coming to an end, and he would have to submit a draft of his article to Scott soon.

After taking several bites of the cold, stale pastry, he tossed it in the trashcan and went back upstairs to his room. He began packing his small duffle bag and pulling together all the loose and random items that had found their ways to the farthest corners of the room over the past few days. Once he felt that he had everything together, he walked downstairs and checked out.

He would make one last stop by Mojo's house before hitting the road, and then it was back to Oxford to write.

It was definitely time to start on his next novel.

MOJO'S DOOR WAS ALREADY OPEN WHEN COLTRANE STEPPED onto the porch. He rapped against the screen door so as to not startle the old man.

"Mojo! It's Coltrane. Just letting you know I'm here."

Not hearing a response, he leaned his head inside of the door and said, "I'm coming in!"

He stepped into the house slowly, his footsteps echoing in the silence. "Mojo?"

Coltrane looked around but didn't see the old man in the main room, so he stepped back onto the porch and looked down the road, both ways. He tried to remember if Mojo had mentioned anything about fishing or going anywhere, but he couldn't place anything.

He stepped off the porch and walked around to the rear of the house. There wasn't much to see back there either, just flat, treeless land extending for what seemed like miles behind the house. He walked back into the house and called out Mojo's name again.

Nothing.

Coltrane considered leaving a note, but then he remembered how Mojo had handed him the record sleeve to read the names of the other musicians on the record. He hadn't wanted to question whether Mojo was illiterate and didn't want to create an uncomfortable situation if, in fact, Mojo was.

He briefly considered going out and picking up a bite to eat and coming back a little later when he thought Mojo might've returned, but decided against it. He walked the full length of the house, checking to make sure that nothing was missing, especially since the door was unlocked. The walk to the kitchen proved fruitless, but as he returned back through the bedroom, something caught his eye: the old man lying motionless in his bed.

Coltrane could feel the temperature around his face getting hotter as he walked over to the bed, calling out the old man's name.

Mojo didn't move.

As Coltrane stood over the old man, he knew immediately that he wasn't sleeping. Mojo's eyes were cracked ever so slightly, unflinching and frozen in time. His rather tall frame appeared small and shrunken in the bed, and although Coltrane knew Mojo wouldn't respond, he shook him slowly, calling out his name. Coltrane touched his arm, and the coldness of the old man's flesh made him pull away quickly.

Suddenly the scene before him registered, and Coltrane felt his heart tug, as if someone had reached into his chest and yanked it down into his stomach. His legs were heavy as he stood beside the bed, sadness starting to cloak him like a wet blanket.

He looked around the small room at all of the things Mojo owned: old worn, but polished, Stacy Adams, khaki and black colored slacks, plaid and striped shirts folded and draped over wire hangers, an old dusty hat that looked like a hybrid between a fedora and a bowler hat, sepia pictures of loved ones grainy from age, and pictures of himself as a young man standing on the rural roads of Mississippi, Ole Annie Mae hanging from his shoulder. This room was where the old man's journey had ended. He didn't deserve to die alone and be discovered by a writer who was just passing through, Coltrane thought. No. He deserved something better, something grander than what could have very well amounted to an anonymous death.

Coltrane reached for his cell phone. Waiting for the phone to ring, he stared at Mojo, the old man's skin glistening as if covered in wax.

"Hello?"

"Erica, this is Coltrane," he said, steadying his voice.

For a fleeting moment, memories of the previous night flooded his mind, but he was brought back into the present as he looked at Mojo, lying still beneath his bed sheets. Holding the phone, Coltrane questioned if he should tell Erica what had happened over the phone, but he didn't see many other options. He briefly considered for a moment calling the police, but he remembered that Rodney was a police officer, so he opted to stay on the phone with Erica.

"Coltrane, how're you? Is everything okay? Last night—"

"Well, actually no, Erica. It's Mojo."

"Mojo?" she asked, her voice full of confusion. "What's wrong?"

He could hear the wheels of her brain spinning rapidly.

"Coltrane, what happened to Mojo?"

He could hear the knot in her voice, the knot that preceded tears.

"I came over this morning and found Mojo in his bed," he responded, staring at the old man.

"Oh God!"

"He must've passed in his sleep or something."

"Oh God," she said again, as if she would be sick.

"I called you first. I didn't know what else to do."

In the silence that followed, Coltrane could picture her standing there, tears in her eyes. He wanted to reach through the phone and comfort her, tell her that everything would be okay. But he didn't know if he believed that himself.

"Coltrane," she said, her voice slow and somber, "I'm on my way."

ERICA CAME BUSTING THROUGH THE DOOR, HER TEAR-stained face seeking solace in Coltrane's embrace. He held her so closely he could feel the heat of her tears soaking through his t-shirt.

"It'll be all right," he muttered, but he knew they were empty words.

She walked toward the bed and leaned over, placing her hand against the old man's face.

"Mojo," she said, caressing his face, "I'm so sorry." She began to sob, her tears interrupting the rhythm of her speech. "I'm so sorry I wasn't here."

Coltrane placed his hand on her shoulder, not knowing what to say.

After standing at the bed for a moment, she stepped away and into the kitchen. Coltrane followed.

Wiping the tears from her eyes, she removed the cell phone from her purse and called the county coroner.

"They're sending someone out to pick him up," she said, sliding her phone back into her purse.

Coltrane followed her back into the bedroom, and they pulled up chairs next to the bed.

"He had been battling heart problems for a while," she said softly. "He had a heart attack shortly after my mother passed away. That's one of the main reasons I've been trying to keep an eye on him."

Coltrane looked at Mojo, half-expecting him to move, to laugh, to spin some amusing anecdote about a woman he had dated from way back when. Instead, all Coltrane could hear was Erica's soft voice beside him.

"He wasn't supposed to go yet. Not like this," she said, shaking her head.

"I understand."

"No you don't," she said. "He wanted to see his son before he got too sick."

Coltrane considered this for a moment. He didn't know what to make of it. The old man seemed as if he had come to grips with his absenteeism as a father. At least that's what Coltrane had gotten from their conversations.

"They had never met though," Coltrane offered, more as a statement than a question.

"That was supposed to change."

For a moment they sat silently. Coltrane felt himself breathing, as if in slow motion, his long exhalations escaping like air from a pierced tire. He tried to shake the awkward feeling of discomfort bubbling in his gut. Here he was in a room growing warmer by the second, yet the presence of death was so strong that it could have been seated in the chair next to him.

"Can I get you something to drink?" Coltrane offered, eager to leave the room, if only to stretch his legs and feel the motion of his body.

"No, thank you."

"At least let me get you a glass of water."

"Okay," Erica said, as she looked over her shoulder at him, a weary smile blossoming quietly beneath her tears.

He walked back into the kitchen, his mind racing with what seemed like a million thoughts. He could still hear the old man's voice in his thoughts: that low, resonant bass that he had listened to on the porch of the house, that same voice he had replayed numerous times as he transcribed the recordings of the interviews. There were still what felt like millions of questions Coltrane had never had the opportunity to ask.

He filled the glasses and returned to the bedroom, where they waited.

It was only after the coroner had left and the staff at the funeral home had picked up the body that Erica began to speak to Coltrane again. She had been quiet since the moment she saw the two men from the funeral home remove the gurney from the back of the hearse and bring it up the front steps. When she finally spoke, the trembling of her voice steadied with each word.

"I need to go lie down."

"I understand."

She looked up at him. "If you want, you can come over."

He knew she could probably use the company, but the thought of her house, after the previous night, left a bad taste in his mouth. He didn't want to go there again, if he could help it.

He reached out and held her close to him. She laid her head against his chest.

"I'm leaving," he whispered.

"Leaving?" she responded, her voice much louder as she pushed away from him.

"I'm heading back to Oxford."

"You're serious. You're gonna leave me like this?"

"We both know that I don't need to be here right now," Coltrane said. "I can only complicate things."

Erica looked at him, incredulous.

"It's like that?" she said, lifting her head upward so that the tears would not blur her vision. "How can you just leave?"

He didn't have the words to respond, but he held his gaze steady, affirmative in his resoluteness.

"Get your story. Flirt with the local girl. I should've known better than to think you actually cared."

"It's not like that."

"Get the fuck out of here!"

"Erica," he said, reaching for her. "It's not like that."

"Do whatever you have to do, but get the fuck out of here! And don't call me again, you selfish bastard!"

He didn't know if she were merely projecting her anger and sadness onto him or if she really meant it. He wanted to take his words back, to follow her back to her house and hold her until things calmed down, but he knew from the look in her eyes that they were well past that point.

He glanced around the house, taking one last look at everything, his gaze finally resting on Erica's face. She turned away from him. "I do care," he said softly.

Coltrane walked out to his car, taking one last look at the house, his heart aching from the woman still inside. He willed himself to turn the key in the ignition and back out of the driveway.

When he finally pulled into Oxford, he realized that his thoughts were still inside of that small shotgun house in Oak Bluff.

Coltrane could not remember anything about his drive back to Oxford, and he could only scarcely remember lying down on his bed and closing his eyes in the darkness of his bedroom. His curtains pulled, the blackness of the room made it impossible for him to distinguish day from night, and for the next day, he slept, waking only to use the restroom, get a glass of water, and return to sleep. When he finally awoke for longer than ten minutes, he found himself staring at the digital clock on the dresser in front of his bed, trying to figure out if the 7:05 meant morning or night.

He felt out of sorts, still off kilter from the events of two days earlier. When he closed his eyes he could see Mojo's body lying helplessly on the bed. He could also feel Erica's eyes piercing him as he left. He could no longer even remember why it was that he had left in the first place. As he pondered the idea, his stomach tightened. It had not been about Rodney—because that seemed like it happened a long time ago—but Mojo. Seeing the old man lying there had forced him to step outside of himself and ask himself *why*. Why had he been the one to find the old man's body? Why had he been charged with the task of writing Mojo's story? Even more, he asked himself why he had allowed himself to feel those pangs of desire for Erica. He didn't have a single answer. The only thing he knew when the morticians removed the old man's body from the small house was that he didn't belong there. Not anymore.

He was a writer, and his job was to be objective, which he felt he had tried to do. The reality was that things had happened around him that had sucked him in. Seeing the hearse pull away from the house, however, had pulled him back into the real world.

Now, he stood alone in his bedroom, his notes and digital recorder sitting atop the simple ash desk in the corner. He stretched his arms as he turned on the lamp. Before sitting down, he peered through the curtains at the early morning outside his window. Quickly, he closed them and took a seat. Pushing play on the recorder, he began to go through each of the interviews, one by one. As he isolated quotes, he found himself remembering his first taste of moonshine. What he wouldn't have given for another drink with the old man now.

He suddenly stopped the recorder and launched his music player, going straight to his blues playlist. The first song was Muddy Water's "Got My Mojo Working," and the up-tempo drive of the song made him think of Mojo with his wide smile and pearly white teeth, a contrast to the deep lines that formed grooves in his dark skin. He imagined Mojo as a young man running from his responsibilities, a man who made choices that, for better or worse, would resonate throughout his life in painful, wailing strums from an old guitar.

As the music continued to play, and the playlist made its way to Mojo's own music, Coltrane could feel the old man communicating through each note he strummed, each moan he hummed, every pat of his foot against the old wooden floor of the recording booth. They all seemed to call out to him in unison that the music was an extension of the man, and not vice-versa. Mojo had sung his life's experiences into song, coded in a milieu of mystery that could only be understood if you had been knocked on your back before and forced to look up at the world while everything moved on around you. Coltrane pondered if a person could truly grasp the depth of blues music if he had never been drunk, made a mistake that would haunt him for the rest of his life, or gotten his heart broken by someone he had loved with all of his being. Without the experiences that gave rise to the blues, the listener was just a passive consumer, a person forced to isolate each note from its native environment in order to put it on display in academia, celebrating it as an American cultural achievement, while simultaneously turning up a nose at the people whose lives produced the art.

He sat down at his laptop and began writing furiously. His fingers moved in a blur, his head bobbing up and down with the rhythm of the music as he wrote about Mojo, attempting to see the world through the old man's eyes—and eventually his own. He thought about Erica, about the buzz in his belly from the moonshine they had shared, about the powerful ache that pulsed in his jaw from Rodney's fist. He thought about the flat land that looked as if it had been pressed down by the palms of God. He visualized the shotgun house, elevated above the ground, the hollowness beneath the old wooden floor. He could see the old guitar, Ole Annie Mae, its worn neck and fretboard. He could even hear the guitar speaking, it's strings screaming the hard life of a man who had spent most of his life in the Delta, seeking solace in the sounds of his music—solace from the confusion of teen fatherhood, the need to overcome the state correctional system, the desire to avoid the labor that had been his family's lot in this world.

Coltrane continued to peck at his laptop, stopping occasionally to massage his tensing hands. By the time he typed his last word, he felt numbness spreading throughout his limbs.

He sat at his computer for a while, his eyes still blurry from the glow of the screen. He tried his best to read through the draft several times, but it was as if his mind had decided to exit his body. Unable to tell one thing or another about what he had written, he e-mailed the draft to Scott over at *Midnight Jukebox*. Only after he clicked "Send" did he begin to question if he had unintentionally isolated the readers.

Sitting there, he realized that he didn't care either way. He had told the story the only way he knew how, the only way he could.

An ache moved slowly over his body in heavy ebbs causing his arms to swing like pendulums. He stood, stretching his sore frame, and closed his laptop. He reached for his cell phone and pulled up Erica's number. Taking a seat on his bed, he stared at the screen for a moment, half-expecting that it might ring. He sighed heavily, his thumb hovering over the "Call" button so long that his hand began to cramp. When he could take it no more, he closed his eyes and allowed his thumb to fall.

As the phone rang, Coltrane knew he would have little choice but to return to Oak Bluff, if only because there was a part of him that was now committed to seeing this experience through. He could no longer outrun the blues, nor did he want to.

PART II
THE BLUES CHILD

No one told Jason Cobbs that first grip would hurt like hell or that he would be squeezed and rotated like a joystick until he feared his pelvis would pop wide open, spilling his guts into the grass behind the old country store. He had imagined the whole scene would be somehow *different*.

"Am I hurting you?"

"Just a little," he said.

He curled his lips into a smile to conceal the discomfort.

"Oh," she said, letting go. "Maybe we should stop then."

He started to tell her "yes," but reconsidered when he realized this was the closest he'd ever been to *doing it* in his fifteen years of existence. He'd never been touched by a girl before, and while it had been a struggle so far, he knew there was still farther to go. The fact that he had even convinced Shelia Williams to go behind the old closed-down country store with him in the first place was a coup, and he wanted to make sure he took full advantage of that.

He quickly grabbed her hand and prepared himself for round two. This time he helped her move her hand more naturally.

"Like that. Just like that," he said, encouraging her.

Shelia smiled and moved her hand with his. "You like that, Jason?"

"Yep. That's nice," he responded, suddenly anxious about whether or not she would stop him from reciprocating.

He was surprised when she put up no resistance.

She had already told him that her ex-boyfriend had fingered her last summer, but this was little consolation to him now, as he fumbled around in her panties, praying he wouldn't poke the wrong hole. She would surely know that he didn't know what he was doing.

"You okay?" he asked to divert attention from himself.

"Yeah. What's up?"

"Nah. Nothing. I just didn't want to hurt you."

She smiled, momentarily stopping the movement of her hand. "You're so sweet."

He grinned back, feeling the slick stickiness in the fabric of her panties.

"If it starts to hurt too much, I'll let you know," she said, starting up her hand again.

He nodded, closing his eyes as one of his fingers slid into her like a magnet being attracted to a piece of metal. For a moment he felt that he had somehow captured sunshine in his hand. The warmth radiated from his fingertip all the way up his arm. How could she stand walking around with this kind of magic in her pants, he wondered.

Not knowing what to do next, he slowly moved his finger around in a circle. She moaned and leaned forward, kissing him sloppily on his lips, her tongue leaving a sticky sheen across his. He kissed her back, moving his tongue out of the way when she forced hers into his mouth.

"You sure you ain't never did it before?" he asked, lifting his head so that her kisses would fall upon his neck and away from his face.

"Yeah."

That was a relief, because she wouldn't be able to tell that he didn't know what he was doing either. They could learn together. The only difference was that she would think he had already had experience. He could blame all of the awkwardness on her, if and when the time came.

Jason leaned against the back of the store and looked out beyond the sparse trees. For a good hundred yards all he could see was an ocean of cloud-like cotton boles floating in mid-air. They looked almost like snow in the spaces between the trees. The scene might have been poetic, if he were not so nervous.

"You gonna let me stick it in?" he said. His voice was still not as strong as he had hoped it would be. She would surely see through his façade.

"I don't know," Shelia said. "What if I get pregnant?"

"I'm just gonna put the tip in. You can't get pregnant like that."

"For real?"

"Yeah. I gotta put it all the way inside you before that can happen."

She considered this for a moment and then shrugged. "Well, okay then. But you can only put the tip in."

As much as he tried, he couldn't slow down the thunderous pounding of his heart; he could even feel it pulsing between his legs, buzzing like a million tiny wings were tickling him.

He looked out at the cotton field again, hoping to find something that would distract him. He imagined walking up and down the long rows, yanking the stubborn tufts from their boles, heat pushing down on him like a thumb on an ant, all while he slid along a sack larger than his five foot four inch frame. Focus on the cotton, he told himself.

"You okay?" she asked.

"Yeah. Just wanted to make sure *you're* ready for this."

"Just the tip now. Okay?"

He nodded.

This was it. He was about to lose his virginity. Suddenly everything else seemed insignificant, and the only thing he could think about was the look of the wild, unshaved bush that peeped out from behind her pink flowered panties as she lowered them to her knees. With her t-shirt flipped up, just above her navel, she looked sexier than he had ever seen her. He stared at her deep brown complexion, glistening with perspiration from the heat. In gym shoes, she stood the same height as he, but the simple, full curves of her young body betrayed the tomboyish clothing that had, up until that moment, concealed her true shape.

The throbbing between his legs stopped for a moment as he approached her. He wasn't sure how he was supposed to position himself, so he stood facing her.

The moment he pushed his erection through the slickness between her legs, searching again for an entrance, he could feel the tingling and throbbing return with a vengeance. He quickly jumped back, releasing himself wildly into the air—onto her shirt, stomach, and hips. He came so hard that the embarrassment of what had just happened didn't register for a few seconds.

"Really, Jason? All over my clothes! I have to go home with this stuff on me!"

When he was able to open his eyes from the intensity of the throbbing, he could see that she was angry. He hoped she would get over it though, because, after all, it was an accident. In the time it would take her to cool off, he figured he could get the sensation back to try again.

"Is there any in my hair?" she asked, suddenly paranoid that he might have hit her everywhere.

"No."

"You got something I can wipe this off with?"

He stared at her for a moment, looking at her clothes. Then he lowered his eyes to the hair between her legs. He could feel himself beginning to twitch, wanting to get hard again.

"A paper towel? Tissue? Something?"

Suddenly he realized that she was talking to him. His brain unfroze and he responded, "Hold on a sec."

He turned around, pulled up his pants, and ran for the trees. He could hear her voice behind him asking where he was going, but he didn't stop until he reached the field. Yanking handfuls of cotton, he returned to her. He wiped her stomach, unaware of the seeds deep within the tufts.

"Ouch!" she said, jumping away from him.

She reached out and grabbed a few pieces from him and started wiping at her shirt. Frustrated, she pulled up her pants.

"You wanna leave?" he asked, hoping she'd say "no."

"I don't feel sexy right now. Plus, I wanna wash this stuff out of my clothes before it stains."

As they walked back out to the county road, Jason playfully nudged her arm.

"Boy, you crazy," she said, smiling.

He was thankful she wasn't still mad at him. "I don't know what happened back there. Girl, you got skills!"

"I didn't do anything."

"You had me pretty worked up. I think I was too ready. Can you be too ready?"

"I don't know. Maybe."

"Can I tell you something?" he asked. "But you gotta promise not to laugh."

"Okay."

"I, uh, I'm not very, uh, experienced."

Shelia smiled, nodding.

"You knew?"

"Not really, but I kind of guessed that you might be," she responded.

"Damn, it was that obvious?"

For a moment his feelings were hurt, but when he felt her nudge his shoulder with hers, he remembered a basic fact that made him feel better: they were friends first and foremost.

"You are pretty sexy," he offered. "I didn't know you were all bodacious and stuff under those clothes."

She blushed. "You really think so?"

"Definitely."

He quietly hoped that she might offer him a similar compliment, but she didn't.

As they approached her mother's mobile home, which was surrounded by a community of other similarly situated mobile homes, he took her by the hand and stopped her.

"Sorry about your shirt," he said.

"Don't worry about it."

He looked away, still embarrassed. "Yeah, well, I just wanted you to know that."

"Please, Jason. It's no big deal."

"Well, did you at least enjoy yourself a little bit?"

She smiled. "It was cool."

He sighed, relieved.

Glancing around the driveway and seeing no car, he asked, "Is your mom home?"

"Nope. She's over in Tunica, working at the Horseshoe."

"What about your cousin?"

"Probably over at the studio getting high."

Jason arched an eyebrow and tilted his head in the direction of her trailer. "Well…"

"Not today."

"For real? Come on. Why not?"

"What's the rush? Plus, I need to do some things around the house before Mom gets back."

"Oh," Jason said, lowering his head and looking away. "Well, when can I see you again?"

"You see me at school everyday."

"No, seriously."

She looked at him for a moment. "I don't know. We'll see."

He watched her sashay up the steps, glancing back at him. Her lips peeled into a smile, just as she closed the door.

Walking the half-mile down the road to his grandmother's house, Jason found his only comfort in thoughts of how sexy Shelia had looked behind the old country store. He reached in his pocket and felt the soft texture of the single, leftover tuft of cotton that had somehow managed to bury itself in the bottom corner of his pocket. As he squeezed it, he, too, smiled.

CHAPTER 15

Ma Bouf's house was small with a faded white surface that looked as if flecks of Delta mud had been blown against it throughout the years and no one had cared enough to wash or repaint it. To Jason, it reminded him of a wrapped up diaper that someone had bowled down a dirt road. It was a far cry from the two-level brick house in Daily he had grown up in, a structure at least three hours east of Ma Bouf's place.

He had always hated coming to the Delta. There wasn't much to do, and everything that he did enjoy doing drew mocking from the kids his age. They ridiculed him, calling him a nerd, green, square, and even lame. To them, he was a walking coochie repellent, a wanna-be white boy always reading books and shit.

Ma Bouf was his father's mother and the only one who volunteered to take him in and keep him out the grasp of the Department of Human Services after his parents' accident. He loved her, which outweighed his disdain for Oak Bluff by a few pounds, he figured.

After living with Ma Bouf for five years, he knew what time she went to sleep each night, what time she took her insulin shots, what days she went to Mt. Olive to worship (and what days he was required to go), and what time dinner was supposed to hit the table. He had carved out a life with her, but he still remembered what it had been like before—when he had the comfort of a room on the second floor of the large brick house. That was his room, not the old guest room he slept in now, the simple room Ma Bouf had in the back of the house, reserved primarily for her quilt-making projects.

He was thankful she had taken him in though, and although he pretended to be too "grown" for her to hug against her hefty bosom, he could count on her being the one good thing in his life. She didn't mind that he liked to read a lot, but she wanted him to do more activities like the other boys his age. "It's good for you to get out there and mix it up with folks," she'd say. At first the process had been slow, but he managed to integrate himself into a small group of two kids from his school, J.P. and Kev, and while he thought they were cool enough, he didn't really trust them. He knew how they talked about other kids, and he figured, if given the chance, they'd talk about him, too. They could never really be his true friends—maybe associates, but never friends.

It was that reason, and that reason alone, that he did not tell them about what happened with Shelia behind the country store when he saw them at school on Monday. He wanted desperately to tell someone about it, but his older cousin Murphy (the only person with whom he had any contact on his mother's side) had already left for basic training. He would just have to keep it to himself.

That night, while Ma Bouf slept soundly, snores growling from her hefty frame in the room down the hall, he called Shelia, anxious to follow up with her and schedule another chance for them to finish what they had started.

"What about after school tomorrow?" he asked.

"I'm s'pose to be getting with my cousin to get my hair did."

"What about the next day?"

"Bible study."

"You got a brotha over here fiendin' like Pookie," he said, using a *New Jack City* reference he thought she might find funny.

"I'll call you."

"It's like that? You're gonna keep me hanging?"

"Boy, you crazy."

He laughed because he felt that was what he was supposed to do.

"Well, just let me know," he finally said.

"If it's meant to go down, it will," she responded.

"If?"

"Anything could happen between now and then."

"That's why I'm putting my bid in now."

"I got you, boo."

Later that night, as he lay on his back staring up at the ceiling fan whipping the humid air around his room, he sensed a tiny bit of hope that everything would work out, and he allowed himself to savor it.

CHAPTER 16

Oak Bluff High School was located on the western side of downtown Oak Bluff, about three miles from Ma Bouf's house, so in the mornings Jason would take the bus to school and walk home in the afternoon. Ma Bouf had told him when he turned sixteen and got his license, he could drive her old Cutlass Supreme to school, but until then, he would have to take the bus or walk. He didn't mind, though. Most of the time he used the walks home to think about whatever he had been daydreaming about during the day. Quite a few of those days were devoted to obsessing over certain girls from his class. The latest and strongest obsession, however, was Shelia.

As he walked out the school building, preparing to head downtown, J.P. and Kev asked to tag along. He didn't mind though. They just wanted to walk around downtown, not walk him back to Ma Bouf's, so he'd still have his alone time to think later.

"Yo, let's swing by the pawn shop. I got my eye on this beat machine they got," Kev said.

"Yeah, we about to put together a demo," J.P. added. "We

didn't think you was into rapping and making beats, J-Cobb, but you can be our manager since you got all them book smarts."

Jason nodded. He could care less about what plans J.P. and Kev had. Knowing the two of them like he did, he suspected there were numerous points at which their idea would fall apart. For one, J.P. couldn't rap, not well enough to charge someone for a CD. But there'd be girls—even if the rap group was wack—and to Jason, the female interest alone would justify the effort.

Navigating the pawn store was like walking through a maze of junk with price tags on it. Jason quickly tired of standing around in the stuffy room and walked outside to lean against the building and wait on the other two.

That's when he noticed the car.

He saw them out the corner of his eye and began leaning to get a better look at the Nissan Maxima parked diagonally across the street. It was definitely Shelia, and she was sitting in the car with Jesse Ray, one of the stars of the high school football team. Because of his angle, Jason could only make out the back of Shelia's head and Jesse Ray's bright yellow, freckled face and reddish hair, leaning toward her. They were too close to be talking. That much was clear.

A lump formed in Jason's throat, and he found that he couldn't swallow. He wished he had never even seen them, that he could just disappear, but then he heard Kev's voice.

"Yo, that's Shelia in there. Boy, Jesse Ray be pullin' them young 'uns."

J.P. nodded, craning his neck to see what he could from his angle on the sidewalk. "You gotta have a ride to pull a female these days."

"She gon' come up now that she fuckin' with a football player," Kev said, smiling. "Wasn't never gon' be 'bout shit, letting all these niggas finger her."

Jason stopped breathing for a moment. He wanted to ask Kev what he meant, but in his utter disbelief, he drifted into a silence that no one seemed to notice. All he wanted to do was go back to Ma Bouf's and lie down on his bed. He needed time alone to fix his thoughts.

"You finger her, too?" J.P. asked, laughing.

"Dude, she done gave a nigga brain at least three times."

Jason blinked and his eyes glassed up. He turned his head, while the other two joked playfully with each other.

"Yo, I gotta take care of some stuff. I'll holler," he said, turning the corner and walking down the street. He wanted to run, but he couldn't let them see him looking so soft. Instead, he walked briskly, as if he had a purpose, and found himself walking toward the downtown business district. Thoughts of Shelia going down on Kev made him want to throw up. He needed to find a place to pull himself together.

Looking down the recently repaved street, Jason saw a decrepit wooden building sitting next to an old renovated train depot. A giant worn-out couch sat just off the entrance of the building. By the time he reached it, he collapsed onto it, no longer able to fight off the tears.

"Boy, you can't be out here sleepin'!" the man whispered, his hushed tone cutting through the evening air as if he were giving away the directions to the Underground Railroad. The man's dark face, covered in thick, matted hair, coupled with two missing front teeth, made him resemble The Wolfman, and Jason jumped, scraping his back against the rough wood beneath the mildewed foam of the couch arm.

"Can't be no sleepin' out here. This here is a place of business," the man said.

Jason blinked his eyes, getting his bearings. It took him a second to remember where he was and why he was there. He stared at the man for a moment, digesting his appearance.

"You a'ight?" the man asked, leaning in closer to examine him. His breath jetted out through the space where his front teeth should have been. To Jason, the smell reminded him of a blend of hot garbage, Budweiser, and cigarettes. He could even feel a fleck of saliva against his nose as the old man spoke.

"Y-yeah," Jason muttered, wiping at his face. And then, for no apparent reason, he blurted out the word "women," as if he had been the pioneer of such a clichéd utterance.

The man nodded, as if the word had far greater resonance than any other word possibly could. "Hey, I'm Sangsta, resident philosopher and expert in matters of the heart."

Sangsta plopped down on the other arm of the couch, extending his wrinkled hand, veins spreading beneath his mahogany skin like the branches of an old tree. Jason gripped it, surprised by its coolness.

"Jason," he said. He was immediately suspicious of the haggard-looking man, so he added, "I ain't got no money."

"Don't want no money, young man. Just wanna show you something right quick."

Sangsta reached into his pocket and pulled out a pair of dice. "Whatchu see?"

Jason said, "Dice. Whatchu mean?"

"What numbers?"

"A three and a five."

"Really?"

Sangsta shook his hand in front of Jason's face, never moving his fingers, as if to wave the dice in front of Jason.

"A three and a five?" he asked.

Jason looked at the dice, baffled. The numbers had changed to a one and four. "What you sellin', man?"

"I'm not sellin' nothing, Jason. I just wanna show you dat everythang ain't always what you think it is."

"Okay. And what does that have to do with women?"

"Boy, that ain't about the women. That's 'bout you."

"Huh?"

"It's all in how you see stuff around you. She ain't do nothin' but be her true nature. What you want her to be, that ain't always who she is. Understand?"

Jason stood up from the couch and looked around at the golden light casting the first shadows of dusk. Suddenly, he was ready to walk home.

"Man, you crazy!" he said, preparing to walk away.

"Ain't never said I wasn't. But you too busy pretending to be someone else that you ain't never gon' be happy."

Jason trotted down the steps of the building, cutting across the parking lot of the train depot, briefly noticing the sign that read "Blues Museum." He didn't have time to stop and listen to that crazy old man. Ma Bouf would be serving dinner soon, and all he wanted to do was return to a place that was more familiar than anything Oak Bluff had to offer. While Ma Bouf's bosom wasn't it, it was close enough.

CHAPTER 17

Jason reached Ma Bouf's house just after sunset. He found her inside watching her favorite television show in the main room. His dinner plate was covered, resting solitarily on the stove.

"Hey, Ma," he said, leaning down and kissing her cheek.

"Gon' in there and get you somethin' to eat," she responded.

He wondered if she could sense his hurt feelings. Maybe she could smell it on him. He had expected her to be angry that he came in after the streetlight came on, but she didn't seem to be bothered.

He walked over and removed the plate from the stove. He was surprised that it was still warm as he placed it on the table. He sat down and started to work on the fried chicken, but his mind began to drift immediately to images of Shelia and Jesse Ray in the Maxima, and then to her messing with Kev and J.P.

He thought back to a few days earlier when he had believed that she didn't have any experience whatsoever, outside of that ex-boyfriend she had mentioned. The awkward way she had stroked him had been proof of that. Or was she messing with his head?

Maybe she was practicing with as many people as she could. He didn't know—and as much as he wanted to ask her what was going on, he fought the urge.

He finished his dinner and kissed Ma Bouf again before heading to his room and lying down. He snuggled against a few of the old quilts and tried to steel his thoughts. He felt his chest beginning to heave, but he refused to allow himself to cry again.

It wasn't supposed to be like this. By now, he should have built a life for himself in Oak Bluff, but every time he put himself out there, he fell flat on his face.

Even worse, he still felt the pain of missing his parents. It was like a cut that never healed.

He missed them so much that his entire body ached from emptiness sometimes. He missed his mother's smile and the way she would walk up to him and squeeze his nose between her index and middle fingers and touch her forehead to his, all the while calling him her little "rascal." He missed the scent of her perfume, the smell of wild flowers showering across his face.

Missing his father was different though. In fact, Jason didn't even know that he could miss his father until the accident happened. He had felt afraid and intimidated by his father, the journalist. The old man's voice was heavy and loud and would rumble inside of Jason's chest when he spoke. Jason admired his father though, the way he strung words together and expressed himself so articulately. Jason secretly hoped to one day embody all of the traits that he admired in his father, but the first thing he let go of when he moved in with Ma Bouf was the very diction he had once so admired in his father. He realized that he was afraid of the taunting of his classmates whenever he spoke "proper" English. The ridicule and occasional scuffles made him long more for anonymity than popularity. It had taken him until last summer to recover from the social stigma of it all, and now that he was fifteen and had a few people who, at least from a public point of view, looked like friends, he was no longer different from anyone else.

But then Shelia came.

He had noticed her sometimes when he went out for one of his walks down the road. He knew that she was a year older than he, but she was more approachable than the other women that he knew, mainly because there was a homely quality to her, solidified by her frizzy neck length hair that appeared thick and Afro-ish in sunlight, although her hair appeared relaxed on the ends. She also wore a pair of glasses and no make-up. Her quiet demeanor was enhanced by the fact that her shoulders were somewhat pinched together with her back curving forward at the base of her neck, giving her a slightly humped over look. Still, there was something oddly cute about her. With one of those makeovers that they did on those afternoon talk shows, Shelia could very well come into her own.

Their friendship had formed loosely around their invisibility at school, and although he would walk over to her house to shoot the breeze two or three times a week, he was largely unaware of what her life was like. That ignorance, coupled with their unguarded conversations, allowed him to think of her as a person like him: misunderstood and alone. When their conversations eventually turned to sex, she admitted that she was a virgin, but was curious about what it would be like to be with a boy. She even admitted to touching herself while in the shower and sometimes at night before she went to sleep. It was only when she revealed that last bit of information that Jason began to see her as a sexual being. From that point forward, he conspired with his raging adolescent hormones to lose his virginity to Shelia.

Lying in his bed, the house absolutely still, save the fan in his room, he had imagined what it would be like to be inside of her: how he would kiss her, how he would touch her.

It took months before he made his move, and when he finally

convinced her to go on a walk with him—that just so happened to go past the abandoned old country store—he had just about mapped the entire scene in his head as to how things would go. When he leaned in to kiss her, she allowed him to. After that, his plan went out the window.

He hadn't expected her to be so aggressive, because in his daydreaming he was the aggressor. When he unleashed his erection into the humid air, he hadn't anticipated that she would grab it so vigorously—or that he would lose control from just being so close to her wetness.

If that level of embarrassment hadn't been enough, hearing Kev and J.P. talk about Shelia, and having seen her with his own eyes in Jesse Ray's car, put everything in a different perspective. Even if Kev and J.P. had been lying their asses off, that wouldn't have explained what he had seen in the car. He thought that he and Shelia were at least close enough for her to be straight up with him about any other dudes she might have been feeling. That's the part that stung the most.

He reached for the cordless phone and held it in his hands, cradling it between his face and his pillow. He debated with himself about whether or not he should call her, but his fingers had dialed her number before he realized it.

Although there was only one phone in Shelia's house, it was not surprising that she was the one who answered it. She lived with her mother, who had recently been hired to work the second shift as a waitress over at the Horseshoe Casino in Tunica, and her cousin Theotis, who spent most of his time smoking weed in a shed-turned-music studio his friends had set up on the edge of town. The moment Jason heard her voice come through the receiver, his stomach tightened.

"What's up, boy?" she asked, her voice light and easy.

"Nothing," he responded, feigning nonchalance.

"How's Ma Bouf?"

"She's good. Just laid down a little while ago."

"Cool. So what you up to?"

Jason considered trading small talk for a minute, but his emotions were still simmering beneath the surface, and he found himself incapable of carrying on an empty conversation. "I saw you today," he said abruptly.

"Yeah, you see me everyday."

"No, I mean I saw you and Jesse Ray."

"Oh."

He had expected her to say more, but as he waited, he realized that she wouldn't.

"That's it?" he asked. "Just 'oh'?"

"What do you want me to say? I didn't know Jesse Ray was going to offer me a ride home today."

"But you were all up on him."

"I wasn't all up on him," Shelia said, her voice curt.

"You were kissing him?"

"And?"

Jason sat up on the edge of his bed, trying desperately to calm his breathing. He couldn't believe that this was Shelia talking to him as if she didn't even know him.

"I just thought, you know, that you and me, you know," he paused. "I just thought that we were taking our friendship to the next level."

She was quiet for a moment, as if to consider how all of this might have affected him. Finally, she said, "Hey, I didn't know you had feelings for me."

"How could you *not* know?"

"I just thought you wanted to mess around. Isn't that all you boys want anyway?"

"I like you," he uttered, feeling suddenly deflated.

As they sat silently on the phone, he considered what she had said and wondered if he hadn't, in fact, been the poster boy for what she had come to expect from guys.

When she didn't speak for a minute, he added, "Do you

like me?"

"Yeah, you're good people."

"I mean, do you like me like a boyfriend?"

"You don't want a girlfriend, Jason. You just want someone you can mess with."

"How do you know what I want?"

"Come on. Be serious. I'm not even saying that we can't kick it anymore. I just don't think we need to be callin' it somethin' it really ain't."

"Well, let me ask you this: who all have you messed around with?"

"Jason, with all due respect, that really ain't none of your business. You just need to worry about how I treat you."

"So you're a ho then!"

"What the fuck did you just call me?" she said, raising her voice.

"You heard me. Just giving it up to any dude in Oak Bluff."

"Motherfucker, you don't know a goddamn thing about me!"

"That's for damn sure! I thought you were my friend."

"You know what, Jason? Fuck you!"

"Yeah, I bet you say that to every dude in Oak Bluff these days."

The click came hard and fast, and Jason was left holding the phone against his ear with a wall of silence forming around him.

As he sat there, his heart racing fast, he considered calling back and telling her off for hanging up on him.

Then after a few minutes, he considered calling back and just apologizing. Things had clearly gotten out of hand. He knew he didn't really mean to call her a ho. He had just gotten angry at her response.

He picked up the phone and called her back, but she wouldn't answer. After two more attempts, he gave up and put the phone down on the cradle situated on the nightstand.

He closed his eyes, a numbness growing across his chest. It

felt like a weight pinning him down to the bed. Unable to move, he realized that the block of numbness was right where his heart was supposed to be.

Loneliness crept over him, and he wished with all of his might that he could just disappear.

CHAPTER 18

By recess the word was out. It had started with some of his classmates looking at him and giggling. Some of them pointed and shook their heads. One kid mumbled "ginseng" to him and walked off tickled with himself. But it wasn't until he met up with Kev right before lunch that he understood what was going on around him.

"Jason. Damn, dawg. You went out like that?"

"Like what? Man, what you talkin' 'bout?"

"They say you wasn't even no minute man. You was a two second brother. They say you ain't even let her get her clothes off before you go skeetin' all over the place."

Heat flushed over Jason's face like scalding water. As the situation dawned on him, he was suddenly terrified of anything remotely connected to Shelia, especially when he considered all of the conversations they had had. Had she really put him on Front Street like that? He knew he had been an asshole last night, but he didn't deserve this. Did he?

"Dawg, they say when you just see the pussy you lose it. Like you could be across the street bustin' nuts on yourself."

Kev seemed more amused than Jason figured a real friend

would have been, but then he knew Kev wasn't really his friend anyway.

"She lyin'," he muttered. "She just mad 'cause I don't want her."

"Yeah, right, Jason. She ain't the girlfriend type, dude. She ain't trying to get with no one on the serious tip. You just got caught out there," Kev said, laughing.

"That girl can't even kiss," Jason said, trying to take the offensive for the first time.

"Who gives a fuck? That ain't got shit to do with getting pussy. Everybody know that."

Kev slapped him on his shoulder, "But on the flip, a lot of niggas wantin' to hit that shit now though. She makin' it sound like her shit so good you couldn't help but bust without hittin' it. Niggas linin' up now. You done put that chick's stock through the fuckin' roof!"

The part left unsaid was that Jason's own stock had plummeted to the point that he couldn't even give it away if he had wanted to.

Jason fumbled through the rest of the afternoon in a daze, avoiding ridiculing glances and smirks and pointed jeers. As soon as the three o'clock bell rang, he eased out the side door and started walking briskly away from the school building. Unable to steel his thoughts, he didn't realize just how far he had walked until he looked up and saw that he was down the street from the building with the huge old couch. Seeing it, he suddenly had the urge to talk to Sangsta. He just hoped that the old man was around.

Rather than plop down on the musty cushions, he opted to walk inside the building. Not knowing what to expect, he found himself standing inside of what looked like a restaurant, old decrepit pool tables grouped near the front door, graffiti written over nearly every inch of the walls by what were probably the customers' own pens. The thick, smoked-honey-barbecue aroma of ribs and chicken filled the air, and he was suddenly ravenous. He dug his fingers through his pockets, feeling for paper, coins, whatever currency might be hidden in the crevices of his natty jeans. His finger brushed lint specks and the key to Ma Bouf's house, but nothing else.

"How many people in your party?" a sprite young redhead asked him.

"Uhh, I'm just looking around."

"Well, we have some really good specials today," she said, proceeding to rattle off a list of delicious-sounding meals so that all he wanted to do was reach over and smack her so that she'd shut up and stop torturing him.

"Thanks" was all he could offer her. "I was supposed to be meeting someone here."

"Oh, okay. Are they here yet?"

Jason looked around and realized he was the only black person in this room that looked like the back alley of a back alley. The only other black faces he could make out were from the kitchen. Seated all around him were white people who looked as if they had walked over from their offices for a late afternoon meal. They sat on the shaky old chairs, bent over cigarette-burned vinyl table coverings, thumbs erect and soaked in barbecue sauce. The scene was a bit baffling, as these people looked more like they would be dining at a country club, not a hole-in-the-wall barbecue joint.

"I don't see him. Do you know Sangsta?" Jason finally asked.

"Yeah. Sangsta has his own table over here," she said, pointing to a table that appeared to be wrapped around one of the beams holding up the roof.

"His own table?"

"Yeah. Take a look," she said, walking him around to the

table. Above the table, affixed to the beam was a picture of Sangsta and President Obama.

"Whoa!" Jason didn't know which one was supposed to be the celebrity in the picture by the way the two men were huddled. "Barack Obama?"

"Yeah. That's really him."

Jason looked around again. He noticed an elevated stage in the back, but he was distracted by all of the writing on the wall and how worn out the building looked. On pure sight alone, he figured the roof would leak if there were even a slight drizzle outside. He had never been inside of a place that actually achieved this level of ragged authenticity. He could have been walking inside one of those dusty juke joints that he had only seen from the outside while walking down the back roads. He had once walked up on a juke joint with Kev and J.P. and peered through one of the cracked windows and seen the dank, raggedy interior. He had wondered why people would pay money to stand around in a place that looked like it was about to fall in. Clubs were supposed to be nice, like the ones on TV, he thought. Now he was standing in a restaurant, a large spacious old building, one that the President of the United States had visited, no less, and he was at a loss for words.

"Sangsta should be here soon. He normally comes in around the mid afternoon," the girl said, pulling Jason out of his thoughts.

"Thanks," he said. "I'll just wait over here by these pool tables."

"No problem. If you need anything, my name is Cindy. I'll be right over here," she said, pointing to a register behind the counter.

Jason turned around and walked over to one of the pool tables. He ran his fingers along the green felt, his fingers catching gritted paint flakes and food crumbs rubbed into the cloth. He wondered how anyone could really play a game of 8-ball on a table that had enough stuff ground into it that a ball could hardly roll straight. As a matter of curiosity, he grabbed the cue ball and rolled it slowly across the table, watching it stutter and jerk across the surface.

"Little man," he heard a voice call out to him.

He looked up to see Sangsta, in all of his rugged glory, ease through the door as if a billion ants were carrying him across the uneven threshold of the restaurant. Jason's eyes lit up.

"Hey, Sangsta. I been lookin' for you."

Sangsta walked up to him and looked down directly into his eyes. "Women, huh?"

"Somethin' like that," Jason responded, tossing the cue ball into the corner pocket across the table. "Somethin' like that."

CHAPTER 19

"So it's like that?" Sangsta said, taking a sip from a bottle of beer and setting it down carefully on the surface of the table beneath his "special" beam. The comment was intended as rhetorical, so Jason just nodded, more as an affirmation.

"Want some beer?" Sangsta said, offering him the neck of the bottle he was holding.

Jason could still see the saliva glistening around the bottles rim. He shook his head.

"My bad," Sangsta said, placing the bottle back down on the table. "I can order you one."

"Nah, I'm good. Dude, I'm like only fifteen."

"Shit," Sangsta said, the word arching across the table like water shooting from a garden hose. "I been drinking since I could stand up and piss straight."

Jason stifled his laughter. Looking at Sangsta, he imagined that the old man had nursed from a forty-liter bottle of malt liquor as a baby. That image made him burst into laughter. Sangsta laughed along, unaware of the joke.

"I'm good," Jason finally said. "What should I do? I can't go back to school. My whole shit is messed up." Cursing made him feel older, and when the old man didn't flinch, Jason reveled in his newfound sense of manhood.

"I'll tell you like this, Jason. Sometimes you da shit, and sometimes you da shovel."

It didn't make much sense, and Jason wondered if it had been a smart move to seek help from Sangsta after all. He wanted the old man to provide him with some nugget of wisdom, some morsel of knowledge that would serve as the antidote for the pain in his gut. In his exasperation, he asked, "So what should I do?"

"Just keep rolling on. You gotta channel that energy into something else."

Damn, Jason thought. The man was making less and less sense. Sangsta looked him over, and he knew that the old man could see the confusion in his eyes.

"What's across the street?" the old man asked.

"Whatchu mean?"

"What's across the street from this here building?"

"I don't know. More buildings?"

"No, little man. Across the parking lot?"

Jason shrugged. "The blues museum?"

"Yeah. That's what I'm talkin' 'bout. That's how you channel the pain."

"What? By going to some museum?"

"Naw. With the blues."

"With music? Man, come on. Music can't change what Shelia did to me."

Sangsta lifted the bottle of beer to his lips again, and Jason watched as the old man's Adam's apple bobbed up and down with each gulp of the remaining brew. Wiping his lips with the back of his hand, Sangsta said, "Blues is the only remedy that I know of for matters of da heart."

Jason shook his head in disappointment.

"It's either that or the bottle," Sangsta said, placing his empty bottle down directly in front of Jason.

Ma Bouf was in the kitchen frying catfish when Jason made it home. The smell of the seasonings was like soft fingertips brushing along the sides of his face, beckoning him forward.

"Hey, Ma," he said, walking over and wrapping his thin arms around her large frame. She patted him affectionately with her free hand and told him to stand back so she could turn the fish over.

Looking at the golden brown texture of the fish, his stomach grumbled loudly. It was bad enough he had sat the whole time at that restaurant and not eaten a thing. Now, being this close to good food made him want to reach directly into the grease and pull it out.

"How long?" he begged.

"Everything'll be ready in a few minutes. Go wash your hands now."

Jason walked back to the bathroom and turned on the faucet. As he ran his soapy hands beneath the water, he imagined Shelia's thin fingers interlocking with his. He wanted to find a way to go back to last night's conversation and tell her that he was cool with just being her friend. He dried his hands, an idea taking form in his head. Maybe he could get Shelia to call off the hounds. Maybe he could get her to be his friend again, and she could tell everyone that she had just been joking. He'd be invisible again, gratefully so.

He walked back into his bedroom, grabbed the phone, and propped himself up against the cushion of two giant half-finished quilts. He dialed her number and tried his best to wait patiently.

After the second ring, someone picked up the phone.

"Shelia?" he said, immediately.

"Naw, nigga. This ain't no Shelia. Who dis?" a heavy voice responded.

"Uh," Jason mumbled. "Uh, this is Jason. Jason Cobbs—from down the street. Ma Bouf's grandson."

"Oh. Well, she ain't here. I'll tell her you called."

Before Jason could say "goodbye," the man hung up.

He couldn't tell whether the man was Shelia's cousin, Theotis, or someone else and decided that he didn't want to worry over that point. He only hoped that Shelia would call him back. He needed her to.

He headed back to the small dining room area, just off of the kitchen. He paced around the table until Ma Bouf told him he could come and serve himself. Dashing into the kitchen he grabbed two full-size catfish and placed them next to a mound of French fries, before sitting back down.

"Say yo grace," Ma Bouf called out to him.

He lowered his head and started praying for Shelia to call him, forgetting all about the food in front of him. When he opened his eyes, he dove into the food. Ma Bouf rarely ate much, and when she did, she would take her food into the den so she could watch her TV shows while she ate. As far as Jason could recollect, he hadn't had a "family-type meal," with everyone sitting around the table at once, since his parents had passed away. He was fine with that, though, because he knew Ma Bouf was sick.

As he finished one side of a fish, he realized just how much he appreciated her. Every day she would cook him breakfast and dinner and rarely enjoy the meals herself. Jason knew she had high blood pressure and high blood sugar and that she couldn't always eat some of the foods that she prepared for him, but he figured he couldn't stop her from making those meals for him—the same meals she had prepared for his father some years ago. To her, this is what a growing boy was supposed to eat, not low-seasoned foods and desserts made with sugar substitutes. At that moment Jason vowed to learn how to cook so he wouldn't be a burden to Ma Bouf anymore. She would say that he wasn't, but he knew, deep down, that he was more a burden than he cared to be. After all, at his age, he should be helping her more so she could tend to her own health.

After he finished his meal, he went into the den and sat down next to her, resting his head on her shoulder. He hadn't done that in a while, and it felt good to feel her soft arm beneath his face and to smell that light scent of coco butter that Ma Bouf used to moisturize her arms.

"You know your daddy used to love to lay his head on Ma Bouf like that, too," she said, her use of third person sounding endearing in a way that only a grandmother could make it.

Jason snuggled against her. She was warm like a quilt that had been lying beneath a window on a hot summer day. He smiled when he thought about his father doing the same thing as a kid. As he thought about his father, he suddenly wanted to know more about him.

He looked up at Ma Bouf. "Ma, what was my daddy like when he was my age?"

She smiled, and as she pondered Jason's question, she suddenly chuckled to herself, her large body rocking, causing his head to bounce lightly on her arm.

"What?" he said, smiling along with her.

"When Melvin was your age he had it in his head he was gonna be one them musicians."

"Like Michael Jackson?"

"Naw, child," she said, chuckling to herself. "He used to wanna be a blues singer."

"Blues? I can't picture Daddy playing the blues!" he said laughing wildly.

"Well, that's what he wanted to do."

"So why didn't he do it?" Jason asked, eager to know how different things would have been if his father had been something other than a journalist.

"We just couldn't get him that guitar he wanted. You know, times were hard, and he wanted this particular guitar. He had seen John Lee Hooker or somebody like that with one of them guitars, and he had it fixed in his mind that he was gonna travel the South playing blues and then go up to Chicago and Memphis and all them other places. It was kinda crazy," she laughed, "'cause he should've been more into that youngster music, like Isaac Hayes and them Earth and Fire people—but no, he liked the blues. See, I used to play them records, and that's most of what he heard growing up."

"My daddy as a blues singer? That's crazy!" Jason said. "Did he ever try to get a guitar again?"

"Naw. It was one of those things. Almost like a phase or something. He wanted one real bad for 'bout a year, and then after that, he discovered girls and sports and all that other stuff."

Jason sat quietly for a moment before saying, "I miss him and Mom."

Ma Bouf wrapped her arm around him, and he felt as if he were being wrapped in a thick blanket of love. "I miss 'em, too," she said, sighing heavily.

~

Lying in bed, Jason looked at the ceiling fan spinning around. He imagined his father and the guitar that his father never got. Then he thought about Sangsta and remembered the old man talking about how the blues was the only way for him to really sort out his emotions. While he had heard a lot of blues music since he'd moved to the Delta, he realized that he didn't really know many details about it. Taking the blues for granted in the Delta was just as easy as being oblivious to the flat land and the cotton fields that populated the area. It was in the air that everyone breathed, like oxygen, but most people never stopped to savor it. Melvin Cobbs had, though. And Jason Cobbs had decided that he would, too.

CHAPTER 20

When Shelia didn't call back, Jason decided to avoid everyone as much as he could the following week. He would give an obligatory "what's up" to Kev and J.P. before quickly whipping up an excuse to be somewhere else. Most of his free time was spent lingering around one of the empty bathroom stalls at the end of the hall so that he could avoid running into anyone. He had even skipped lunch on several occasions. Most of his afternoons were spent thinking about his father and blues music. He had even found some old cassette tapes that Ma Bouf had stuffed in the bottom of a drawer and had started listening to them on the worn-down tape deck in the room, which, incidentally, was the only part of the old stereo that even worked, the record player having died so long ago that he had never seen a record anywhere in the house.

On several days he went downtown to find Sangsta at the restaurant (he later discovered it was called Mack's Shack). They would chat, and Sangsta would offer to buy him a beer—never food. They'd chat about heartache and music, but he had yet to work up the courage to tell the old man that he was considering learning to play the guitar. On the days when he didn't go to

Mack's Shack or straight home, he would look around at some of the pawnshops he had previously avoided and check out whatever guitars they had available. He had walked inside a music store once, but he felt as if he did not belong. With no money, he reasoned that he didn't have any business inside of the store in the first place. He had even walked around the gift shop at the blues museum, but because he didn't have the money to view the exhibits, he resigned himself to strain and see what he could from the gift shop.

When he went home, he would lie on his bed and listen to Muddy Waters and Howling Wolf and John Lee Hooker, the men whose names were written along the sides of the tapes, and there were others, but the names of those singers were not on the tapes' labels. Within days, he had begun to memorize the songs and pantomime the guitar parts, developing a respectable air guitar. He had even taken to placing a thimble on the pinky finger of his left hand, and he pretended to wiggle the finger against the fretboard of his imaginary guitar, like a bottleneck sliding across the strings. The lyrics washed over him, and while he couldn't understand everything that they were singing about, he could sense a lot of it, and that bit that he understood directly made him feel like even more of a man.

One night while sitting in silence in his room he thought he could hear the soft moan of a guitar singing out in the distance. He sat up in his bed and listened. The guitar sounded almost like a woman's voice, but he knew it was a guitar. He smiled. The sound of it was so beautiful that he wanted to be inside of it. He lay down on his bed and closed his eyes.

He thought about his father lying in the same bed many years ago, and he wondered if his father had heard the guitar singing in the distance, too.

When he came to Oak Bluff five years ago to visit Ma Bouf for a week during the summer, he had no idea that he would never leave. The visit had been a yearly routine where his parents would drive him over to Oak Bluff to spend some time with his grandmother while they took some "couple's time" to go be romantic with each other. Jason didn't mind though. He always felt funny when he saw his father grab his mother's behind and squeeze it, while she smiled. Sometimes he would walk in on them kissing heavily in the kitchen. So having them take a week to do whatever it was that they did when he was not around, especially since he didn't want to walk in on them and see something he definitely didn't want to see, was fine by him.

Jason had actually enjoyed being around Ma Bouf, although he found the town of Oak Bluff itself a bit underwhelming in comparison to Daily. Ma Bouf would make it better for him by driving to Wal-Mart when he arrived and buying him a toy to play with while he was there. She would cook delicious meals, and at night, after he put on his pajamas, she would let him lie down across her lap while she scratched his back. The back scratching was her secret weapon. She had it down to an art form where she could scratch with her fingertips in such a way that it caused the areas outside the range of her fingers to itch, which would make him squirm all over her lap until she had to scratch every inch of his back to complete and total satisfaction.

It was on a Wednesday afternoon, while he was playing in the front yard with his G.I. Joe action figures, when he heard his grandmother scream out. It was the most horrific, piercing sound he had ever heard, and he jumped to his feet, afraid to approach the house. As he walked cautiously toward the front door, he listened carefully, praying that Ma Bouf was okay. He opened the door slowly and found her doubled over on the couch crying with such intensity that he immediately began to cry, too.

"Lord Jesus!" she wailed. She rocked back and forth, shaking her head at the phone that rested on the coffee table in front of the couch.

When Jason was close enough to her, she grabbed him and pulled him to her. He was immediately swallowed in her warm arms and sweeping sadness. He cried, but didn't know why.

"Baby," she said, holding his face with her strong hands. "Help me, Jesus!"

Suddenly Jason felt his stomach tighten. The fear that struck him at that moment would have killed him had his grandmother not been holding him.

"Baby, your parents…"

She couldn't finish the sentence.

She didn't have to.

FOR WEEKS AFTER HE LEARNED OF HIS PARENTS' CAR accident, he couldn't sleep by himself. He slept next to Ma Bouf in her bed, pretending to be asleep, but thinking about the last moments of his parents' lives. He had memorized the story and read every newspaper article on what had happened. His parents were coming across Arkansas on Interstate 40 East, headed back to Memphis and then on to Daily, when a trucker driving an eighteen-wheeler fell asleep and the trailer came across the line on them. To avoid crashing into the truck, Melvin Cobbs had slammed on his brakes and angled his car toward the shoulder of the road, but another car tailing too closely behind him didn't respond quickly enough and plowed into them. The effect was that Melvin and Diana Cobbs were swept completely off the highway and down a steep hill where they slammed into a series of trees, wrapping the vehicle around one tree and lodging it between another.

The damage to their bodies was so severe that Ma Bouf and Jason's mother's family members (who had fallen out with his mother ever since he could remember) argued for two days over whether or not they should have an open casket funeral. Ma Bouf knew that she didn't want people to see her son propped up in his casket with wax filling in his face. While she felt that Diana was her own daughter, and not merely a daughter-in-law, she found herself in a heated argument where one casket would be open at the funeral while the other would be closed. The dispute was only resolved when a tear-soaked Jason had appeared during the hottest part of the argument to plead for his mother's casket to be closed, along with his father's. Feeling embarrassed and ashamed of themselves, his mother's family acquiesced to Jason's wishes, and shortly after the funeral, they slithered back to where they had come from, leaving him alone with Ma Bouf. The only member of Jason's mother's family who attempted to maintain contact with him was Murphy Jenkins, who would come and stay with Jason in Oak Bluff at Ma Bouf's house for a week or two each summer. Now Murphy was in the army, about to be deployed.

Life had changed dramatically in those five years, and Jason thought that he was doing much better. Still he missed his parents. Sometimes he would start crying out of the blue. It was as if he yearned for some lingering connection with them. Those tapes had been a gift he hadn't anticipated. Now through the music, he was able to connect with his father, and through his father he was connected to his mother, by touching the dream that his father had so long ago. At that moment, he wanted to grow up and become a bluesman.

It was an early Saturday afternoon when Jason heard the sound of the guitar cutting through the quiet space of the occasional passing car on the narrow country road. He recognized it immediately, like the coco butter scent of Ma Bouf, and he headed down the steps of the house and started walking toward the sound. He feared the sound would lead him down towards Shelia's trailer, but as he walked the road, he looked down a side road and was able to spot an old man sitting on the porch of a narrow shotgun house playing an old brown guitar. Jason walked up to the old man's house, standing at the base of the steps of the porch while the man squeezed out the last note of his song.

"I'm Ma Bouf's grandson," Jason volunteered.

"I know you," the old man said matter-of-factly. "You sellin' somethin', son? I don't do that ganja no more, so you gotta take that shit down the road."

"No, sir. I don't mess with that stuff. I'm fifteen. Ma Bouf ain't having that."

"Sir?" the old man laughed. "Yeah, I can tell you some of Miss Bouf grandson. She used to put that 'stension chord on yo daddy when he showed out. She believe in keeping her folks in line." He chuckled and sat the old guitar down, leaning it against the house.

"Yes, sir," Jason said, smiling. "You play a mean guitar!"

"You ain't gotta keep calling me 'sir.' I ain't gonna tell yo grandma!"

The old man lifted up the guitar again and placed it across his lap. "Come on up here, boy. What's yo name?"

"Jason Cobbs."

"I'm Morris Jones, but folks 'round here call me Mojo."

Jason lips spread into a full-toothed smile. He liked this man immediately.

"You know how to play the gee-tar?" Mojo asked, handing the guitar over to him.

Scared and excited, Jason held the guitar, admiring its faded brown wood. It looked as if it had been played on for more years than he could imagine. He loved the way that the wood of the guitar's neck nestled into his left palm. "No, sir. I don't know the first thing about playing this here."

"Well, you gotta hold it like so," Mojo said, taking the guitar from Jason and balancing the curve of the guitar on his right knee as he lifted the neck with his left hand. "See? Like this here. You gotta hold her just right if you want to make her do her thang for you. A'ight, now you try."

Jason pulled up the other chair on the porch and sat down next to Mojo. He tried his best to hold the guitar in the same position that the old man had.

"Just relax, boy. All that tensin' up shit gonna make her not wanna give you none."

Jason laughed and tried to relax his posture.

"Okay. Now place this finger here and this finger here. Okay. Now hold down those strings and strum it with your right hand."

Jason did as he was told, and smiled broadly when he heard the sweet sound of his first chord.

"Now look at yo hands. You got it?"

Jason nodded.

"Okay. Now, give me the gee-tar."

Jason handed the guitar back to Mojo, who promptly returned it to him.

"Now play what I just showed you," Mojo said.

Jason took a deep breath and repositioned the guitar on his lap. When he placed his fingers on the strings and strummed, a horrible sound rumbled out of the instrument, nothing like the beauty he had just played.

"That ain't it. Try again."

Jason moved his fingers and strummed again. The noise seemed worse this time. He quickly stared at the neck of the guitar and repositioned his fingers and strummed again. The dissonant sound jarred him so badly that he stopped cold.

"Forgot that quick, boy?"

Embarrassed, Jason nodded.

"You gotta find them strings. Do I need put some hair around them strings for you to find the holes?"

"Huh? Whatch mean?"

"Take it you ain't never had no pussy. How old you say you is?"

Feeling the nervousness in his stomach building, he swallowed hard and responded, "Fifteen."

"Yeah, I was 'bout fifteen when I got my first piece. Two dollars for the girl, and two dollars for the room," he laughed.

Jason laughed, too. He might have been a virgin, but at least his first encounter with sex was free.

"A'ight. Hold up the gee-tar. Push down these two strings right here," Mojo said, pointing to the strings.

Jason pushed down the strings and strummed with his right hand. The beautiful chord came back.

"Look-a-here," Mojo said. "I ain't no gee-tar teacher, but if'n you get a gee-tar, I'll try to show you some of these old blues licks."

"Thank you, sir."

"Enough with that 'sir' shit!"

Jason jumped at the man's voice. "Okay. No more 'sir.'"

Mojo smiled at Jason, and Jason smiled back.

As he walked back down the road, he practiced pressing down those two strings in his mind. He promised himself he would never miss that chord again.

CHAPTER 22

With Sangsta and Mojo, Jason felt as if wisdom was within reach whenever he needed it, and that feeling of having men around him who had experienced life made him feel as if he were on firmer ground than he would have been listening to Kev and J.P. making fun of him one minute, then treating him like a friend the next. That confidence propelled him to call Shelia again. This would be his last phone call to her. If she wasn't trying to hear anything he had to say at this point, even after he apologized, then he would just let the issue go. After all, he would have done all that he could've done to repair the situation.

Around ten o'clock that evening, he picked up the cordless phone next to his bed and held it to his chest. He listened closely to see if Ma Bouf was asleep. When he heard her snores rattling from down the hall, he took a steady breath and dialed Shelia's number. The phone picked up this time, and he waited for a voice to say "hello," rather than jump the gun like he had before.

"Hello?"

It was definitely Shelia's voice, and that made Jason's heart beat faster.

"Hey, Shelia. This is Jason."

Silence.

"Shelia, you there?"

"Yeah," she said dismissively. "Whatchu want?"

"Hey, it's just," he paused and took a deep breath. "It's just, you know, I wanted to apologize to you. That's all. You and me, we've been good friends, and we've been through a lot, you know? I know that I haven't always been the best friend to you, and I'm sorry for that, but I never stopped looking at you as my friend."

Silence.

Jason continued, "I've been thinking about how we used to talk on the phone and go walking. I miss hearing your voice. And then I called you and left a message and never heard back from you, so I figured you weren't even trying to hear me."

"What message?"

"I left a message like a week ago. A dude answered the phone. He said he'd tell you I called."

"Damn Theotis," Shelia said.

"What?"

"That nigga didn't tell me a thing. Why didn't you call back?"

"I thought you didn't wanna talk to me."

"Jason, now you know my cousin is always high. How did you expect him to give me that message?"

"I don't know. I guess I thought he would write it down."

"Please. Theotis? He too sorry for that."

Jason smiled, sensing the inkling of some relief.

"So you say you miss me?" Shelia asked.

Feeling a little more confidence in his voice with the darkness of the room cloaking him, he responded. "Yeah, I miss you."

"So why did you call me out my name?"

"Kev and J.P. told me some stuff about you."

"Oooh, I hate them! Liars! Both of them!"

"Really?"

"I hope you don't believe anything they told you."

"So you didn't mess with them?"

"Hell to the no! We used to play when we was in elementary school, and I remember one time we played that 'show me' game where everyone took down their pants and showed what they had. We were kids just playing around. That's the only time them niggas been near me like that."

Jason laughed. "Shit, they had me goin'."

Then he remembered the kiss in the car.

"So what about Jesse Ray?"

"So we tryin' to tell all our business tonight?"

"I just want to make sure we're still friends."

"You know you talk kinda proper when you get serious," she said, chuckling softly.

He laughed along with her. "So are you going to tell me or leave a brotha hangin'?"

"I had been feelin' him for a while, and that day you saw us, he was giving me a ride to the library. Before I got out the car, he pulled me close to him and started kissing me."

"And you kissed him back."

"Well, it ain't like I got a boyfriend or somethin'."

Jason was quiet for a moment as he relived the feeling of hurt in his gut when he saw them. "So are you all a couple now?" he asked.

"Please. All boys are alike. All they wanna do is get you alone and see how much they can get from you—and when they can't get what they lookin' for, they break out, like 'see ya'."

The notion came over Jason very slowly, and he didn't realize exactly what he was saying until he heard his own voice. "You're still a virgin?"

"You supposed to be my friend, and you keep sayin' foul stuff to me. What kinda girl do you think I am? Of course I am. You would've been my first if you had-a acted right."

"I can act right," Jason offered quickly.

"Yeah. Whatever. Just like all them other boys," she scoffed. "You just tryin' to get you some."

"No. It's not like that. I really do like you."

Shelia was quiet for a moment.

"Don't play with me, Jason. I ain't into no games."

"I wouldn't do that to you."

"You really feelin' me? For real for real?"

"For real for real."

"So what now?"

Jason looked out the window and saw the glowing street post. "I feel like I need to see you right now."

"Boy, Ma Bouf would snatch a knot in yo ass if she caught you goin' out this late."

"Let me worry about that."

"So you gonna come over here?"

"I can do that."

"You ain't gettin' none tonight, if that's what you thinkin'," Shelia said.

"That's cool. I just wanna see you."

"So you about to come right now?"

"Yeah."

"Well, be careful walking along that road."

Before he could hang up the phone, he could hear Shelia say, "Boy, you some kinda crazy!"

THE STREET LAMPS WERE SPACED OUT SO WIDELY THAT THE half-mile walk was done almost completely in the dark, with Jason using more memory than actual sight to navigate his way to the trailer park. As he approached the nook leading to Mojo's house, he noticed the silhouette of the old man sitting in the darkness while talking to another man. The shapes had scared him for a moment until he realized that they were having a conversation.

He didn't know if the old man could make him out from that distance, but he stuck to the darkness along the road as he continued to walk.

When he finally made it to Shelia's trailer, all of the lights were out, and he immediately wondered if she had fallen asleep. He knocked softly on the door and sighed in relief when she opened it. Shelia was dressed in a large t-shirt that looked like a nightgown, and her hair was pulled back into an Afro puff. She didn't have on her glasses either, which allowed Jason to see how beautiful her eyes really were. For a moment she stood in the doorway looking at him.

"What's wrong?" he asked.

"I'm just thinkin' if I should let you in."

Jason's brow furrowed. "I just walked all this way to see you."

"I know. But I'm just saying. If I let you in here, you gotta promise you won't try anything."

"I promise."

"Jason, I'm serious."

"I said I promise."

"Okay."

Shelia parted the door, and he eased through the crack into the living room area. He followed her over to the couch in the room, barely able to see without the lights on, but he didn't want to ruin the mood by complaining.

The couch was located right under a window covered with heavy white blinds and a thin sheer curtain so that the mild illumination of a street light in the distance created a bit of a glow in the darkness, allowing him to make out the curvaceous features of her body. Damn, she was fine!

For a moment they sat in silence looking at each other, and Jason wondered if he should say something, anything to make this moment a bit more magical.

"So what's up?" she said, positioning herself in the glow of the streetlamp.

"You."

"Oh really?" she said leaning in closer.

"Yep," he said, as their lips met. He had expected her to swallow him with one of her wet kisses, but she didn't. Instead she allowed her lips to become soft and sweet against his, brushing her tongue softly against his as they kissed. He figured that she had altered her technique since her brush with The Upperclassmen, but he let the thought go as he enjoyed the feel of her mouth against his.

Reaching out in the darkness, he touched her breasts, feeling their warmth and softness beneath the thin shirt. He wanted her so badly that he could feel his erection pressing angrily against his pants.

As he moved his hand down her stomach and towards her panties, she placed a hand over his, stopping him.

"Why not?"

"Not yet."

"But I want to touch you."

"And you will. Just not now."

She leaned over and continued to kiss him.

Again he tried.

"You persistent, ain't you?" she said. "Just wait a few days, and we can pick up where we left off."

"Why?"

"Now just ain't a good time. You have to trust me on that one."

Slowly, he began to understand what she was hinting at. He didn't mind that they would have to wait though. He just wanted to hold her close to him and enjoy the feeling of being held in return.

He wondered how all of this would play out at school, but as he felt her snuggle against his chest, he realized that he didn't care what anyone else thought.

Jason sneaked back into Ma Bouf's house without being detected. In fact, not even Mojo was outside when he made his way along the dark country road in the wee hours of the morning. He tiptoed into his room and collapsed on the bed, the cordless phone still lying on the bed, right where he left it.

He thought about Shelia's kiss. Then he thought about the sweet sound of the chord he had learned.

He smiled, taking in what it felt like for things to finally start to go right for a change.

The first cool day of fall caught most of the kids off guard. Even Jason had already stepped outside the house before doing a quick u-turn and heading back to get a jacket. The cool air whipped at him teasingly, as if to say that it would be hotter than two field mice fucking in a wool sock later in the afternoon, but that he'd have to take a jacket with him for now. The cotton was disappearing by the day, with only the random cotton bole left standing. The machines had been working over time to get the crop up, and the fields now looked like they would have after a partially melted snowfall.

For a change, he decided to go back through his normal routine of moving about the halls of the tenth grade, without regard to potential ridicule. At first some people giggled at him, but those few who did giggle sounded like the last people to get a joke that was already old and stale. Shortly before recess, while at his locker, Shelia walked up to him and kissed him squarely on the lips, where people could see that they were now an item. After that, people left him alone. After all, if Shelia was good with Jason, then the joke had clearly run its course. Plus, with the growing male interest in her at the school, guys started nodding their heads to Jason when he passed, a nonverbal salute to his being the guy who had succeeded in taking her off of the market. While it seemed as if he was the only benefactor from this newfound relationship, he noticed that Shelia maneuvered more easily through the throngs of girls at the school. The fact that she had hooked up with a guy removed some of the tension she had caused among the other girls, and they had begun to show their appreciation for that.

In Jason's mind he imagined that things could get no better. He vowed to call Shelia later and to go by and tell Sangsta the great news about his new relationship. By the time he arrived at Mack's Shack and situated himself on one of the two stools at Sangsta's special table, he could hardly contain himself. He strained to be patient while looking around at the graffiti-filled walls. He had come to think of them as a second home. In fact, he had memorized several of the phrases on the wall, along with their exact locations, and even though he knew in the back of his mind that they would be there, he still found himself double-checking when he sat down. Maybe there would be a new word or phrase. He honestly believed that he had memorized certain sections of the wall where he could easily identify any new markings in the cacophony of penned and markered print and scribble. He had even learned how to shoot a billiard ball straight on the old pool tables, and although the sticks had chalky, worn down corks on the tips, he felt that he was now a part of the home team, the team that could play on such a table and win.

Sangsta floated through the door around a quarter to four that afternoon. The old man walked on the balls of his feet, almost on his tips, pushing off of the ground with each step, a walk that would have made identifying him from any distance quite easy. Sangsta smiled when he saw Jason and took a seat across from him in the usual spot.

"I see somethin' done changed in you," Sangsta started. "It's been a minute, but I think I can tell when a man in love. You in love, boy?"

Jason smiled and lowered his head, his blushing inhibiting his ability to speak.

"Well, good for you."

Sangsta signaled the server to bring him a beer. He nodded at Jason.

"I'm good."

"Just checkin'."

It was their ritual, one that involved lamenting broken hearts, celebrating life, savoring the blues, and, in Sangsta's case, downing a few beers in the process.

"So tell me about this girl," Sangsta said, taking a huge swallow from the ice-cold bottle that had just been placed in front of him.

"It's Shelia."

"The same Shelia what broke yo heart?"

Jason nodded.

"I see you's gonna be a true bluesman, boy!"

Jason laughed, but didn't know why. "What do you mean?"

"It mean you just got on that rollercoaster of love. It's the same one all bluesman done gone on. See, to really understand blues music, you gotta understand that it start, just like ole Son House say, with a man and a woman. The man gotta love that woman for there to be somethin' there—and she gotta love him real hard right back."

Jason nodded to disguise his confusion. Was Sangsta telling him that Shelia was going to break his heart again? He wondered if she could do that to him. It didn't seem like she would—but that didn't mean that she couldn't. He shook his head. Maybe he was thinking about Sangsta's words too hard. Maybe there was something simpler buried within them.

Jason finally opened his mouth. "Do you think she's gonna break my heart?"

"Naw. I think she gonna treat you the way you treat her."

"So what's the deal with this Son House/blues thing?"

"You'll understand what I mean better by and by."

"Man, I hate it when grown folks say that."

"That's because you still young, and you feel like you know everything. I know. When I's yo age, I thought I had everything down."

"But I don't think I know everything."

"Well, let me try to put it to you this way, boy: for the blues to matter, you have to have cared really hard about someone."

Right when Sangsta said that, Jason had a thought that struck him like a bolt of lightning. "Does it have to be a woman? I mean, can it be like your parents or something."

"The way I sees it, Jason, it can be about anyone that you done loved. Ole Son was thinking about a man and a woman, but I think if you got some hurt deep down in yo heart, no matter who they is, you got the blues."

Jason nodded solemnly.

"But you tell me 'bout this Shelia. She pretty in the face and thick in the waist?"

Jason laughed. "She's fine."

"And she yours, too, ain't she?"

Jason smiled, "Yeah, I guess you could say that."

"Well, don't be shame then. Say that shit out loud! Say 'she my woman, and I loves her!'"

In a low, soft voice, Jason said, "She's my woman, and I love her."

"I can't hear that shit, boy. 'She my woman, and I loves her!'"

Jason giggled and tried again. "She's my woman, and I love her." This time he was a little louder.

"Louder, boy! Louder! Make this whole place know you in love. And stop saying that shit all proper like. Just let it come out of yo soul. 'She my woman, and I loves her!'"

Jason stood up out of his chair and closed his eyes. "She my woman, and I loves her!" he yelled, hearing his voice bounce of the walls of the entire restaurant. He opened his eyes, and ignoring all of the customers' eyes looking at him, he grabbed Sangsta's beer and took one long gulp, before slamming it down on the table. "Dammit," he said, with no fear in his voice. "She my woman, and I loves her!"

BY THE TIME JASON MADE IT HOME AND CHECKED ON MA Bouf, he was already out the door heading down the road to see Mojo. He felt like he had a lot of things that he wanted to say, but these weren't things that he could say with his mouth; these were things that he could only express through music. The more he knew about how to play the guitar, the better he would be at letting these things come out of his soul.

As he walked up to the house, he saw a woman walk out. He knew that was the woman who took care of Mojo—actually everyone in the community knew. Ma Bouf had once told him about her when they had driven past the house one day and saw Mojo and the woman on the porch.

"Mr. Jones used to date that young girl's mother. He stuck with her through some tight times too, took care of her when she got sick—right up until she died. I think that girl is just repayin' the favor."

While Jason looked at the woman as just Mojo's caretaker, he couldn't help but notice how attractive she was. She had to have been at least ten years older than he, and to a fifteen year old, that might as well have been twenty years older. Still, he enjoyed seeing her on those rare occasions when their paths crossed.

The woman pulled off in her car by the time Jason made it into the yard. He walked up and knocked on the screen door of the shotgun house. The door behind it was already cracked halfway open.

"Hold on," Jason could hear Mojo saying from the back of the house.

"It's me, Mr. Mojo!" Jason called out through the screen.

"Ma Bouf's boy?"

"Yes, sir!"

"Be right there," Mojo called out, a slight strain in his voice.

Jason paced around on the porch for about a minute before Mojo eased his way out onto the porch. The weather had warmed up substantially from earlier that morning, and the old man was wearing a short-sleeved button-up shirt with suspenders. In his right hand was a cane, which he had used to push the screen door open.

"I'm starting to feel the music building up in me," Jason said.

The old man nodded. "You get you a gee-tar?"

"I've been looking, but I have to be honest: I don't have any money."

"Is that yo excuse?"

"If I don't have any money, then how am I supposed to get a guitar?"

"That's for you to find out."

Mojo sat down very slowly in one of the two chairs and leaned his cane up against the house. "I'm not as young as I used to be."

Jason nodded, still distracted by the old man's last comment.

"How am I supposed to find out?" Jason asked.

"Young blood, you say the music building up inside you, like you 'bout to bust, but you ain't tryin' to find that gee-tar to let it out. Sound like you ain't really 'bout to bust then. When you want somethin', you do whatever you gotta do to get that some-thin'. No 'scuses. You understand?"

"So, I should get a guitar, no matter what?"

"If that's the way you feel 'bout it."

It seemed almost as if the old man were playing some kind of game. Jason knew that Mojo understood his situation. The best he could do was ask Ma Bouf for a guitar for Christmas and hope like hell that she actually bought him one. He couldn't hold out that long. Did Mojo really expect him to? Maybe this was like a riddle and he was just thinking about it all the wrong way. After all, the only person Jason knew who had a guitar was Mojo. If he couldn't buy a guitar, he would have to beg someone for a job and pray that they didn't hold his age against him. It was either that or just steal a guitar, something that he was unsure if he could do. Even if he were inclined, he couldn't just walk into a store and slide a guitar out under his jacket.

Frustrated, Jason asked, "Do you have any suggestions to get the money?"

Mojo shook his head. "I won my gee-tar off a poker game. The ways I figure it is this: if you meant to have a gee-tar, you'll have a gee-tar. One will find its way into yo hands—if it's 'spose to happen."

"Well, can you at least show me a few more chords before I head home?"

Mojo went to stand up, but grimaced hard. "You can go in there and grab the guitar out my bedroom. It's in the corner. I can't be using my strength up goin' back and forth gettin' stuff."

"Okay," Jason responded, opening the screen door and walking into the house.

"And don't be lookin' at none of them magazines on the dresser neither!" he could hear the old man call out behind him.

Jason had never been inside of a shotgun house before, and he was surprised to see everything in one straight line. From the door, he could see all the way to the kitchen in the back of the house, yet there was no hallway. One had to walk through each room to get to the back of the house, since they were arranged adjacent to each other with the door frames lining up so that you could see through each of the rooms. The first room was a living room kind of area with old chairs off to the side. There was even an old record player up against the wall. The next room was what he assumed was the bedroom. The bed sat off to the side, and the arrangement of the room was such that he almost forgot that there were door frames on either side, splitting the room in two. The walls were a drab brown with a hint of a yellowish tan mixed into the square-like patterns. There was nothing attractive about the room, but it looked comfortable all the same. It was definitely the room of someone who had probably been around when such a style would have been fashionable. The thick smell of fried bacon and empty beer cans hung in the air, and Jason wondered what it was like for Mojo day-in and day-out in the house. Out the corner of his eye, he saw the guitar propped up in the corner beside the window. As he lifted it, he felt as if he were being reunited with something powerful, even transformative, on some level. Carrying it out to the porch, he handed it gingerly to Mojo and took a seat next to him.

"You remember that chord I showed you last time?"

"Yes, I do."

Mojo handed Jason the guitar, and Jason positioned it on his lap and situated his fingers on the fret board. With his right hand, he strummed the guitar and smiled when the beauty of the chord caressed his ears.

"Okay," Mojo said. "I hear you there, young blood."

Jason smiled, rubbing his hand across the smoothness of the guitar's worn wood.

"Now hold these strings down here. Yeah, like that. Now here's the tricky part. You gotta only play these strings. Can't play all of them or else it's gonna sound like shit. Try that right quick."

Jason fumbled with the strings for a few seconds, but quickly found his chord. He played it several times, and when he felt that he had internalized the chord, he played it in combination with the other chord he had already learned.

"You hungry, ain't you?"

"Yes, Mr. Mojo. I really want to learn this song."

Mojo showed him the last two chords of the song, and Jason

played them over and over until he felt that he could make it through the song without messing up.

"Are there any words to this song?"

The old man laughed. "There some stuff I been known to sing to it, but there really ain't no words. You just sing what you feel to them chords right there. You make it up as you go along."

"Kinda like freestyle rapping?"

"Like what?"

"Like when rappers make up their raps while they are performing them."

"You know Ole Mojo don't know nothin' about no rap music."

Jason smiled and started to strum the guitar.

The sun began to set across the flat land, leaving its orange and red hues lingering in what was left of the blue sky. Jason gazed out at the dusky evening feeling a calmness come over him. His fingers were talking. They only knew four chords, but they were still speaking those four chords as best they could.

"Hold on," Mojo said.

Jason stopped and looked at the old man. Noticing that Mojo was looking at the road, he turned to see the woman in the car from earlier returning to the driveway.

"She gon' need some help with them groceries."

"No problem," Jason said, hopping down off the porch and walking over to the car.

"Thank you," the woman said as she stepped out of the car and opened the trunk.

Jason smiled and reached in grabbing two of the bags. By the time he had gotten to the porch, Mojo had managed to work himself up on the cane to open the door for him. He walked briskly through the house, feeling the weight of the groceries pulling at his arms. Placing them on the table, he turned around to see the woman holding two more bags. He quickly helped her with them.

"Thank you! Aren't you sweet," she said. "What's your name?"

"Jason, ma'am."

"Well, I'm Erica. Nice to meet you, Jason."

"Nice to meet you, too," Jason responded, smiling.

They walked back onto the porch, and Jason noticed that there was now another car in the yard. He turned to see Mojo standing to shake the hand of a brown skinned guy with a low haircut. What had started out as just he and Mojo working on some music had suddenly become a crowded group in only a few minutes.

"This here is Jason," Mojo said.

"Hey," Jason said, extending his hand.

The man shook his hand. "Good to meet you, Jason. I'm Coltrane."

"He a writer. Come to do a story on Ole Mojo."

"Cool!" Jason said.

"We 'bout to get started, so you and me gon' have to finish up later. Okay?"

"Okay."

"Tell Ma Bouf I said 'hello.'"

Jason could hear the men beginning their conversation as he walked out to the road. Looking around, he thought briefly about walking farther down to see Shelia, but he could still feel the tips of his fingers vibrating from the strings of the old guitar. He moved his fingers along his imaginary fret board. The music was still dripping from him, and all he wanted to do was put his hands on a guitar.

Before he knew it, he found himself back at Ma Bouf's, lying against a pile of quilts in his room, staring longingly at the ceiling.

He tried to steel himself, but he couldn't. He could still hear the music.

The idea had come to him late that afternoon, and for the rest of the day, he twisted the idea around in his head, looking at it from every conceivable angle, weighing all of the pros and cons. The problem was that it all made too much sense to him. He needed a guitar. That much he knew. He also knew that it would take forever for him to earn the money necessary to purchase a guitar. But it was Mojo who had told him to do whatever it took to get a guitar.

Unable to sleep that night, he lay on his bed, his stomach nervous with the realization that he was close to acting. He glanced at the clock and noticed that it was nearly 2:30 a.m. Could he actually pull this off? Part of him felt like he could, but the other part of him felt that, not only would he not succeed, what he was thinking of doing was plain wrong. It was at times like this that he wished he had Murphy there to talk to him. He wondered what his cousin would tell him. He wondered what Sangsta would tell him. He didn't want to know what Ma Bouf would tell him.

The window had been slightly ajar. He remembered noticing that. The way he figured it, he wouldn't have to go all the way in;

he could just reach in and grab it. He would just be borrowing it anyway.

Maybe the old man would admire his commitment to learning the instrument. But what if he got caught? He didn't know if there were any guns in the house. He would hate to come in through the window only to get shot in the face. But the old man was having trouble getting around. He wouldn't have enough time to chase him if he was even awake. Jason couldn't remember there being a gun next to the bed, but he kept telling himself that if there had been, he would have noticed.

Even if he was able to get the guitar out of the house, how did he expect to bring the guitar back over to the man's house to practice in his face with his own stolen (or in the loosest sense "borrowed") guitar? Jason liked Mojo, but he had begun to fall in love with the guitar. If he took it, he would have to keep it hidden at home until he could figure out something. Maybe he'd just hold on to it long enough, until he was able to get another guitar. He would definitely give it back. After all, he was no thief.

STANDING IN THE NEAR PITCH-BLACKNESS OF THE DELTA night, Jason, dressed in a black sweatshirt and sweatpants and a black toboggan, hunched against the side of Mojo's house, just under the window to the bedroom. Sweat collected in the elastic knitting gripping his forehead. Part of him wanted to go back home and forget this crazy idea; the other part of him wanted the guitar so badly his fingers tingled with expectation.

He crouched on one knee against the house, his body obscured by total darkness. The closest house was more than fifty yards away, and all of the houses along the road were dark so that only their outlines could be made out from the distant street lamps that sat just off the road. Jason waited silently, listening for any sounds from inside the house.

After what seemed like an eternity, Jason realized that he either needed to get the guitar or go home. It would be foolish to let the sun rise on him while he waited, cowering in the shadows, deliberating. Slowly, he rose to his feet, sliding his fingers beneath the windowpane that was still slightly elevated. Inch by inch he lifted the window as slowly as he could to not make a sound. When he got the window up as far as he could reach, he realized that he hadn't calculated how much higher up the window would be because of the elevation of the porch.

Panic seized him for a moment, but he quickly gripped the windowsill and lifted himself off the ground. While suspended in mid-air, he continued to ease the window up very slowly. Once he was able to see more clearly, he noticed the old man in the bed, undisturbed, totally unaware of his presence. With a slight grunt, Jason reached over beside the window and wrapped his hand around the neck of the guitar. Steadying his hands, Jason lifted the guitar, careful not to bump it against the windowpane. With all of his forearm strength, he raised the guitar parallel to the floor and even with the window. The weight caused his arm to tremble beneath the strain, but the adrenaline pumping through his veins gave him the last bit of strength to pull the guitar toward him through the opening in the window.

Just as he eased the guitar alongside himself, his eyes, now more adjusted to the darkness of the room, cast as glance at the old man lying in the bed.

"Oh shit!" Jason uttered quietly under his breath. He pushed himself back and fell onto the ground, his arms blanketing the guitar like a newborn. Without thinking, he ran toward the road, toward the darkness, his feet barely touching the ground. All the while, he listened keenly for the sound of the old man yelling or the cocking of a gun.

With the house disappearing behind him, he strained to hear anything other than the thumping of his own heart. Even the crickets had seemed to stop chirping. He stopped when he reached Ma Bouf's driveway. He listened again. Silence.

Sitting on his bed, Jason stared at the guitar and a chill came over him. Had the old man seen him steal the guitar? Maybe he would come to Ma Bouf's in the morning and tell her about what Jason had done. Maybe he would come knocking on the door as soon as he could get out of the bed and get down to Ma Bouf's. Maybe he would come around to Jason's own window. Jason's mind raced. Anything could happen now. He instinctively reached over to make sure his window was locked.

Staring at the guitar for a moment, he quickly slid it beneath his bed. He couldn't stand to look at it any more. It was as if he had brought a haint into the house. Peeling his clothes off and tossing them on the floor, Jason hid under one of the quilts, unsure if the goose bumps forming on his skin were from the autumn night air giving way to morning or from the guitar that rested corpse-like beneath his mattress, its voice strangely mute.

The following day, as Jason moved about the school, he felt as if he were being watched—followed. The only time that he was able to sit for longer than five minutes without shifting his weight uncomfortably was when he met with Shelia during recess. He wasn't very talkative, and she didn't press him. She only asked if he was all right, to which he responded that he was, although he hadn't slept much. As she sat there, he wanted to tell her everything that had happened last night, but he didn't understand the nature of the events himself. Why had he been so reckless as to steal the guitar? Even as he sat trying to push his thoughts further from the event, he found himself remembering the old man lying there. He still wondered whether the old man had seen him.

"Well, when you wanna talk, just let me know."

"I will," he said, leaning over and kissing her.

After school let out, he headed down to Mack's Shack in search of Sangsta. Surely Sangsta would understand what he was feeling: the confusion, the excitement, the desire to be as close as possible to the music until it became a biological and natural extension of yourself. Sangsta was the only person he could think of who might be able to help him shift this burden from his chest and, although he hated to admit it, tell him what the right thing was to do in this situation.

When he walked through the door of the restaurant and headed over to Sangta's table, he was met by Cindy, the young woman who always served that particular table.

"You looking for Sangsta?" she asked, taking her ordering pad out of the back pocket of her jeans, although she knew that he would not be ordering anything (since he never had any money).

"Yeah. Just wanted to talk to him when he got in."

"He won't be in today."

"What? Is he okay?" Jason suddenly asked, beginning to panic at the mere thought of something tragic having happened to his friend.

"Yes. As far as I know. He had some family business to attend to and left for Chicago yesterday."

Jason wondered how the woman had come to know so much about Sangsta. From her wording, he sensed that she knew a bit more, so he asked her, "What happened?"

Cindy pondered for a second as to whether or not to tell Jason, but as she looked at him, his eyes pleading for anything she could share with him, she responded, "I think his daughter is going through a divorce or something—but you didn't hear that from me."

"Man," was all Jason could muster before stepping down from the stool and walking out onto the elevated landing where the couch sat. He didn't even know that Sangsta had a daughter. At that moment he realized that there were a lot of things that he didn't know about his friend, and that left a hollow feeling in his gut. The feeling was more the result of his realizing that their friendship was largely one directional, with all of the help and advice coming from Sangsta to Jason. There was nothing that Jason had offered in return to his friend, other than problems that he felt needed solving. And it seemed that his problems were nothing in comparison to the problems that Sangsta's own daughter had been facing. He suddenly felt a blend of shame, loneliness, and the inevitable self-pity that seemed to ease upon him in his moments of sadness.

The walk home was long, and the wind picked up, whipping at his face as he walked. At several points, he had to bend over to hold his small frame firm so that he didn't blow away. By the time he reached Ma Bouf's house, his feet ached. It was as if he had never walked that path a million times before. This time, however, it felt like he was carrying weight on his shoulders as he took each step.

He climbed the steps slowly and walked into the house. He found Ma Bouf's note on the table saying that she had gone to see a church member from Mt. Olive at the hospital. The note told him he could warm up some leftovers if he became hungry. Placing the note down, he continued on back to his room, closing the door behind him. He quickly reached beneath the bed, pulling out the guitar and laying it across a quilt that had been spread out over the single-size frame.

He stared at it, examining the craftsmanship of the instrument, its strange, worn beauty. He ran his fingers along the wood, as if caressing a lover. He didn't want to give the guitar back—not yet. But the gnawing in his gut made him realize that he would have to part with it very soon, if he didn't want to cause any friction between Mojo and Ma Bouf in the foreseeable future. He considered that he would sneak the guitar back through the window he had taken it from the previous night. He could then go over the next day and talk to Mojo and offer a formal apology and do whatever it would take to get back into the old man's good graces. Maybe he'd offer to run errands, maybe even cut his grass in the spring—whatever it took to get the old man to trust him again.

Jason stepped outside onto the porch and looked around. The wind was letting up, and he decided to walk down the road to see

Shelia. He would keep an eye out for Mojo sitting on the porch of the old shotgun house, but he didn't know if he had the courage at the moment to actually approach him.

As he walked down to the road, he noticed that there were hardly any trees along the road. He remembered that there were trees everywhere, especially out in the country, when he had lived in Daily. The Delta was different though. It was just a lot of flat lands and fields. Even with the houses being spread out, there was nothing much to look at. To truly appreciate the area, a person had to know someone already there or have a fondness for the absolute plainness of the Delta landscape. Suddenly Jason wished he could fly, soar up above the spacious green land and go somewhere—anywhere—else. He began to run as fast as he could. He only slowed when he came within striking distance of Mojo's house and saw several little kids standing in front of the house, their bikes laid flat against the ground. Several cars filled the narrow driveway.

Jason cautiously walked up to the kids. "What's going on here?"

"Mr. Jones dead."

Jason shook his head in confusion. "What did you just say?"

"Mr. Jones dead. They say he died in his sleep."

Jason rushed up the steps and beat on the screen door. Erica appeared in the doorway, her eyes red as if she had been crying for hours.

"Jason," she said, opening the door and reaching out to embrace him.

He hugged her back, although he still could not comprehend what was happening. "What happened?"

"He passed in his sleep."

"No!" Jason yelled. "He wasn't supposed to die!"

The tears came down his cheek so quickly the sensation terrified him. He quickly pushed away from Erica and darted down the steps. He ran and ran, his feet guiding him aimlessly. He couldn't think. He had no idea of where he was until he lifted his hand to knock on Shelia's door.

When she opened the door, he grabbed her and held her, unable to control the trembling of his body.

"Come in," she said, offering him a seat on the couch in the living room. "Talk to me, Jason."

"He's dead!"

"Who's dead?" she asked, rubbing his hands in hers. "Jason, breathe for me, baby. Breathe. Talk to me."

"Mojo, I mean Mr. Jones."

He had mentioned Mojo to her only a few times in passing, but in that area of the county, everyone knew everyone else. Jason was the only one who was discovering each of the residents on his own.

"My mama told me about it before she went to work. That's so sad. They say he died in his sleep."

Jason wiped his eyes, wanting to lift the weight from his shoulders. "Can I tell you something? But you gotta promise me that you won't tell anyone."

"Sure, baby. I got your back."

He inhaled deeply. He was unsure if he wanted to tell her everything, but he decided that he had to tell her everything if he wanted to free himself of the weight.

"I broke into Mr. Jones's house last night and stole his guitar."

"What? What are you talking about?"

"Late last night I crawled in through his window and took that old guitar of his. I don't know why. I just had to have it. When I left out, I saw him, and I think he might've saw me, too." He started crying again. "I think I killed him when I took it."

"What? No. No! You didn't kill him. He died in his sleep."

"Because I stole his guitar!"

He leaned over, yielding to her hug.

"Baby, you didn't kill him," she said, but Jason wasn't sure if he believed her.

"What do I do?" he asked, standing up.

"Baby, there's nothing to do. You didn't do anything."

"Yes, I did."

Shelia stood up next to him and took hold of his hands. "You didn't kill him. I will put that on anything."

"I don't know."

Shelia lifted Jason's face so that they stood eye-to-eye. Caressing the sides of his face, sweeping away the tears, she gently kissed him on his lips. He allowed himself to melt into her kiss, feeling his shoulders lighten. The warmth of her face felt like the dawn sunrise sweeping over him, and he gave himself up to the sensation.

"It's gonna be okay," she said in between kisses. "You're a good person."

He savored the taste of her lips. "I love you," he heard himself say, before he realized it.

"I love you, too," she responded so quickly, it seemed intuitive.

He stood absolutely still for a moment, allowing everything to rain down over him, everything that had happened since he had returned to Oak Bluff this last time. He could feel the emptiness from the loss of his parents, Mojo, and even Sangster. He was alone, and the feeling was scary.

He had to remind himself that he still had Ma Bouf and Shelia. There were still people around him who loved him. That didn't make the pill any easier to swallow, though. He could still feel his stomach throbbing with the ache of loss. Surely he would survive all of this. He would find a way to transform all of his pain into music. He had to.

He looked into Shelia's eyes, wanting to find solace in them. There was something soft, resting just beneath the surface, but he couldn't touch it—just yet. It was the promise of a promise or the notion that the world would one day be different. He wished that day would flash-forward so that he could experience it *now*.

"Everything is gonna be okay," she said, holding his hands in hers.

"Everything is gonna be okay," he repeated.

"Yes. It will."

He closed his eyes for a moment, willing himself to believe those words with every ounce of his being.

PART III
THE BLUES SON

Putting down Princess had been something he had desperately attempted to avoid for more than a month. When the dog's suffering became so noticeable that Ike Jones could feel the pain himself, he had his wife, Diane, take little Rachelle to the mall for a "ladies day out," while he and Princess shared the somber drive over to the vet.

Looking into the rearview mirror that he had adjusted to see the backseat, he watched his Scottish terrier lie on her side, too exhausted from pain to even whimper. Ike shook his head. He wasn't ready to let go just yet, but he knew that allowing the dog to linger on like this was far worse than being selfish—it was cruel.

Princess lay there, her black fur, once shiny and radiant, now dull and lifeless. Ike felt the tug in his chest, remembering when he had picked up Princess as a pup. She had been the runt of her litter. He knew he had wanted her then. She was the one that the Jones family would love and shower with affection. Princess had been with him and Diane two years before Rachelle was born, and now that Rachelle was eight, Princess was regarded as another member of the family, albeit one with thick, curly hair and a penchant for wagging her tail against Ike's leg as he read the evening edition of *The New York Times*. Although he had asked Diane to take Rachelle out as a distraction from what he was about to do with Princess, he now felt that *he* was the one who needed the distraction.

By the time he arrived at the vet, he had begun to question whether or not Princess could make it another week. He looked at her, longing to hear that robust bark of hers instead of the weak, breathless whimper that had become her way of communicating. Gathering her into his arms, he looked up and away from the vet assistant approaching him. With his arms outstretched, Princess hanging limply, Ike was unable to wipe the tear that made its way slowly down his cheek.

Princess went quietly, without a struggle.

Walking somberly back to his car, Ike wrestled with the emptiness burrowing its way deep into his chest. He inhaled deeply and stared at the brick structure in front of him. He knew he would have to give Rachelle the talk about "death," something he had been dreading. He knew as she became older there would be other speeches: the more detailed talk about sex, the talk about race and how there are still some people who would dislike her because of her dark brown skin, and the talk about how some men could potentially treat her differently because of their backward views of women. He would make sure that she was aware of how special she was and that, although some people might one day behave unfairly towards her, she was still capable of achieving any dream that she could create in that beautiful mind of hers. But the death conversation would come first.

He pulled into the driveway of the two level brick house he had purchased for his family five years earlier. He had thought that Parsippany, New Jersey, was too far from New York to be an effective commute on a daily basis, but several things had happened since they moved there. After a reasonable bus commute for roughly a year, Ike's side business, a consulting practice he did with database system maintenance, began to take off, so he left his job in middle management at an insurance company where he oversaw a team of claims representatives. He didn't particularly enjoy the work, but it had paid the bills. In the meantime, to make use of his bachelor's degree in business information systems, he had begun the lengthy and somewhat painful process of getting various certifications and had lucked up when a friend who worked at a small, private investment banking firm hired him to consult on a database administrative system they were considering. Things went well, and he found himself with a growing client base. When he was able to match his salary at the insurance company, he promptly issued a two-week notice. He had not looked back since. Instead, he ran his business from a large room that had been converted into an office and spent most of his free time enjoying the closeness of his wife, daughter, and perky Scottish terrier. It was the life that he had always wanted, one that he thought would be denied him, given the struggles of being reared by his mother, a woman who had fled Mississippi, long before he could remember, to go to Chicago to stay with family when she had become pregnant. He knew only his father's name, never having met the man at any point in his life. When his mother passed, shortly before he and his family moved to New Jersey, he had vowed to be the best father and husband that he could be so that would be the legacy of his family name, as opposed to the mess that his absent father had created.

As Ike walked into the den and took a seat in the large recliner in the corner of the room, he reached for the remote control. He needed something to take his mind off of the speech he would soon give his daughter. The room suddenly seemed too quiet. He missed the jingle of the nametag around Princess's neck and the quick shuffle of her feet against the hardwood floors. He pressed the power button and began flipping channels, finally stopping on an action movie that he had watched twice that month already.

Leaning back, he closed his eyes and exhaled deeply. His family would be home soon.

CHAPTER 27

The phone rang, jolting Ike from his sleep. He lifted his head slowly, listening for Diane or Rachelle to answer it. When the phone continued to ring, he arose from his recliner and went to the cordless phone that sat on a charger at the edge of the room. Diane was probably calling to let him know they were going to pick up something for dinner.

"Hello?"

"Hello. Can I speak to Mr. Isaiah Jones?"

"This is he."

"Mr. Jones, this is Julius McWilliams. I have some news for you concerning your father."

"Father?" Ike responded. Had he heard correctly? He had distinctly heard the word *father*. "Mr. McWilliams, I don't have a father."

"I'm sorry to be calling you like this. I guess I should have stated that I am with McWilliams Mortuary in Oak Bluff, Mississippi. Your name was given to us as the only surviving family member."

"Well, I don't know who told you that. I don't have a father. Never did."

Ike hung up the phone, holding it tightly in his palm as it hung at his side. He could scarcely understand what had just happened. His father? Dead? He had never met the man in his entire life. As far as he was concerned, the man did not exist anywhere except on an old folded birth certificate buried in the bottom of the personal documents Diane kept in their private vault. He tried to convince himself that he could care less about anything that Julian McWilliams had to say about that. He wanted to, but the call had actually stoked a set of smoldering coals that he thought had gone out a long time ago. He shifted his face and exhaled deeply, before walking back to his chair.

The phone rang again. His stomach dropped as he considered that Mr. McWilliams was trying him again. Glancing at the caller ID this time, he was relieved to see Diane's name on the screen. He quickly answered.

"Is everything okay?" he said before Diane could utter a word.

"Yeah," she responded. "Just wanted to see if you wanted me to pick you up anything to eat while we were out."

"Oh," he said, relieved.

"Are *you* okay?"

"Yeah," he said unconvincingly. "It's just…well…nothing. But yeah, pick up whatever you want."

"How did everything go with Princess," she asked.

He knew that she had to have been standing next to Rachelle, because he could hear her voice attempting to conceal a greater concern for their fourth family member.

"She went quietly."

Diane was silent on the other end for a moment, and a stiff lump appeared in Ike's throat as he considered how such news would affect his wife, even with her having known what was going to happen.

Ike broke the silence by asking about Rachelle.

"She's fine. We've been talking. She knows that Princess is sick and about her age making it difficult for her to get the kind of treatment that would make her better."

"Mommy, is that Daddy?" he could hear his daughter asking enthusiastically.

"Yes. This is Daddy? Want to speak to Daddy?" Diane asked.

"Please!" the little girl said, her voice dancing with expectation. She was truly a daddy's girl, Ike thought, smiling.

"Hello," he said in his happy father's voice.

"Hey Daddy!"

"How has your day been?"

"Great! Mommy found me the cutest purse."

"Nice," he responded.

Then out of the blue, Rachelle asked, "Is Princess all right?"

Ike froze, unsure of how to answer the question. He didn't want to tell her the news about Princess over the phone, but then again, he and Diane had agreed to keep their lying to their child to an absolute minimum—especially on things that she had a right to know.

He chose his words carefully. "Princess is no longer in pain."

"She's dead."

His daughter's words had come so plainly and bluntly, without intonation, that his fatherly instinct took over, and all he wanted to do was hug his daughter and help ease her out of the shock he had inadvertently caused her.

"Well, yes—but it's okay," he responded. "She's in a better place."

"I know," Rachelle said, sounding much older than her age. "She was a good dog."

"Yes, she was."

He could feel relief dawning over him as he realized that Rachelle was not as distraught as he thought she would be. It also made him realize that maybe he and Diane had underestimated their daughter's ability to understand something as heavy as death.

"You know I love you, right, baby?"

"Yes, I love you, too, Daddy!"

"Okay. Put your mother back on, please."

He could hear Diane taking the phone. "She's growing up so fast."

It wasn't a question, but Ike agreed. "I love you," he said.

"I love you, too."

A smile dancing on his face, he realized just how happy his family made him.

"See you in a few," he said.

As he hung up the phone, he could feel a warmth in his chest; he and his wife had managed to avert a potentially distressful situation and had actually been all the better for their loving bond.

Sitting in the recliner, he couldn't fathom what he would do without his family. The thought filled him with joy, but that joy quickly shifted to confusion when he thought about his own father. He knew of the man. His mother had answered all of the questions that she could for him as a young boy, but now, as he stared at the cordless phone, he wanted so desperately to have talked with his mother more about this man before she passed away from cancer. Instead, he knew only that his father was a blues singer in Mississippi and that the old man had never put forth the effort to come visit him in Chicago or send a birthday card or come to a graduation or make any kind of effort to be a part of his son's life. He was nothing more than a sperm donor. Still, on a frustratingly simple point, if it had not been for Morris Jones, he would not exist, and as much as he would like to deny that very issue, he could not. That man's absence had shaped the man that Ike had become. While he couldn't calculate it, that bit of reality had some currency.

Sluggishly, he walked back to the cordless phone and checked the caller ID. He dialed McWilliams Mortuary, not even realizing that he was still exhaling until after the man on the other end had said "hello" for the second time.

Even after everyone had finished the pizza that Diane had brought home, Ike was still contemplating the phone call that he had had with Julian McWilliams. The young man's voice had been steady and reassuring, as if he had those types of conversations everyday. Not knowing how to feel about the situation, he had asked Julian if there was anything owed on the funeral expenses to which the young man had replied, "Everything has been taken care of. We were just instructed to notify you of the date and time of the service."

"By whom?" Ike had asked.

"Erica Townsend, a young lady who had been taking care of Mr. Jones."

Ike didn't know who Erica Townsend was or what her relationship had been to the old man, nor did he care. Apparently she, or someone else whom he did not know, was going to pay for the funeral. He wondered for a moment why anyone would even bother to call him. He was actually surprised that anyone even knew of his existence—after all, he did not know much of anything about the man who had died.

Sitting in the great room, Rachelle sitting between him and

Diane as they looked at the giant flat screen television, he wondered if he would go. Could he go? Could he actually bring himself to travel all the way down to Bumblefuck, Mississippi, where they probably still lynched black people at the courthouse square? All of that to see a man he had never met? He knew he was capable of many things, like starting his own business, but he did not know if he had it in him to pretend to care about Morris Jones. Even though the old man was dead, he still could not shake the desire to whisper a violent "fuck you" to the corpse.

Brushing his hand across his daughter's head, he wondered if he would even tell her that her grandfather had just passed away. She would not know who the man was or what he looked like or even have a memory of being given a toy or spare change by the man. Morris Jones was not even a part of Rachelle's world. He never existed. In fact, Hannah Montana was more real to her than Morris Jones would or could ever be. Not even Diane had known about the old man. His absence had been so total and deafening that he had ceased to be a part of any meaningful conversation throughout the ten years that Ike and Diane had been married. Diane knew that Ike had a father only in the sense that a human being knows that it takes two people to reproduce. Ike considered whether he would even mention any of this to her. His family was already in tact, and he wondered what kind of effect this new bit of information would have on them.

As he considered whether or not to share the news with his family, Ike became momentarily bothered. At a time when he should have been focusing on the loss of Princess, here he was entertaining thoughts of a man he had never known. The irony of it did not relinquish its grasp over him: he cared more about his dog than he did his own father. It was the kind of thing best left unsaid for fear that such a declaration would be considered misguided at best and absurd at worst. But he could not help how he felt. At that moment, he felt more inclined to attend any makeshift funeral Rachelle might have wanted to have for

Princess than he would any funeral for the man who had helped to bring him into existence in the most technical sense of the words.

Lying in bed with Diane later that night, after tucking in Rachelle and hearing her pray for Princess's soul, Ike blurted out the news of the phone call.

"Your father? Your *real* father?" she responded, differentiating between Ike's biological father and the man who had been Ike's mother's boyfriend for roughly ten years until he was accidentally shot to death by a young gangster who had been aiming at someone else.

"Yeah, the man on my birth certificate."

"Oh." She reached out and rubbed his arm. "I'm so sorry, baby."

"No need to be," Ike responded. "It wasn't like I even knew who he was. He was just a name on some paper."

"Yeah, but he was still your father."

Ike exhaled slowly, choosing his words carefully. He did not like talking about this kind of stuff with his wife, and he did not want to respond callously to what was just her attempt to be empathetic to his situation. "My mother was both my mother and my father. He was never there. He wasn't even there when we got married. He doesn't even know that you or Rachelle exist. He didn't even know if I was alive."

"Baby," Diane said, rubbing his arm.

"He didn't give a shit about us. We didn't even exist to him."

She said nothing, only reaching to hold his hand. She always did that when she realized that there was nothing she could actually say to make him feel any better.

"So the funeral is on Saturday in Oak Bluff, Mississippi."

"Are you gonna go?" Diane asked, her voice soft and sweet.

"At first, I was thinking that there was no way in hell I would go down there. But part of me just wants to lay eyes on this guy before they put him in the ground. I just want to see him. You know, see if he had a nose like mine or ears like mine. I want to know who he was and why he didn't want me and my mother."

He could feel his eyes beginning to glass up, but he refused to shed a single tear for Morris Jones. He would not allow himself to feel enough to even visit those emotions.

"I can check plane tickets tomorrow," Diane offered.

"If I go, I have to go by myself."

Diane nodded. "I understand."

"I just don't know if I want you and Rachelle to even bother creating a space in your hearts for this man." He shook his head slowly. "I don't even think I could tell Rachelle about him, let alone take her out in the middle of lord knows where to see the dead body of a man she has never even heard of."

Diane nodded again. This time she sat in silence as she watched her husband wrestle with his thoughts.

"I mean part of me is saying that I need to stay here and forget that I ever got that phone call. The other part of me is hoping that by seeing this man, I can close a chapter in my life that has been open since I can remember. But that's what I feel *I* need, not something I would want to carry past me on into another generation."

"I could come with you, baby. We could let Rachelle stay in Brooklyn with my sister."

"I just think," Ike said, pausing and carefully measuring his words. "I just think that I need to do this by myself and just get this out of my system. Alone. I mean, I don't know how I'm going to feel when I look at his body. I might want to hit him. I might not feel anything. I don't know. But whatever I feel, I want to know that it's just me getting square with him in my own way."

Ike rubbed Diane's hand while he continued. "If it were anything else, I would want you right there by my side. But this? This is some other shit. All I can think about is my mother telling me that my father would never be a part of my life. He was a bluesman, she told me. And you know what? I never allowed myself to even listen to a single blues song. I didn't want to accidentally hear his voice on something, because I didn't want to know that he could be okay without me in his life. How could a man pick a career over his family? What kind of man would do that?"

"Well, you're not that kind of man. You're a wonderful husband and a wonderful father."

"Thank you," Ike said, leaning over and gently kissing his wife. "No thanks to my own father though."

"Baby," she said. "It's because of your father that you have made yourself into a man who would put his family first. It took him leaving you for you to become the man that you are."

Ike listened silently. He knew that she was right, but admitting it seemed to be an indirect way of giving credit to this man who was never there.

Ike leaned over and kissed his wife again before turning off the lamp beside the bed. He knew he would travel the distance to Mississippi to see his father's body, but what he did not know was if such an act would actually bring the kind of closure to that part of his life that he so desperately longed for.

CHAPTER 29

The flight into Memphis International Airport had been uneventful, which was a pleasant thing as far as Ike was concerned. He couldn't remember having ever been this far south before, and he could feel his pulse quicken as he stepped into the terminal. Carryon bag in tow, he walked along the buffed linoleum floor observing the grayish-brown bricks lining the corridor. Somewhere out there in the distance was the lifeless body of the man who had drawn him here, and he was now more uncertain of his trip than he had been while sitting in the comfort of his Parsippany home.

He had decided to rent a car, since the drive to Oak Bluff would take roughly an hour. His compact car—and to call it compact was actually generous—awaited him just outside of the airport, its buffed gunmetal gray gleaming in the October afternoon. The temperature was slightly warmer than Parsippany but still a bit breezy. He quickly popped open the trunk and put his bag in, reaching in his pocket for his cell phone, which he had just remembered to turn on.

"Hello?"

"Hey, Diane. Just wanted to let you know that I made it."

"Good. Did the flight go smoothly?"

"Well, I'll just say that I didn't wake up from any turbulence."

She chuckled. God, he loved the music of her laughter.

"I'll call you when I get checked in."

"All right. You be safe, baby."

"I will. Love you."

"Love you, too."

"And kiss Rachelle for me."

"You know I will."

He sat down in the driver's seat and slowly fastened his seat-belt. Taking a deep breath, he placed the key in the ignition, punched the address of his hotel in Oak Bluff into his GPS, and braced himself for what awaited him down the highway.

IKE BARELY REGISTERED THE CHANGE IN LANDSCAPE AS HE drove deeper into the Delta. When he finally focused, he realized that he was driving down some of the plainest highway that he had ever seen. With all of the trees along the New Jersey Turn-pike, he had never imagined that a highway could exist with nothing running alongside it. It was as if the sky had opened completely over the road like an endless blanket of soft blue. Out of pure awe, he almost pulled over and took out his camera to document it, but quickly decided against it, eager to get checked in.

As he continued on, his radio turned off, his mind drifted again. For the first time since he was a teenager, he actually contemplated what had happened with his parents before he was born. His mother had told him that you couldn't be pregnant and unmarried back in those days in Oak Bluff. Why hadn't his father married her, he had asked. "He was just a kid. He was probably scared," she responded. She described her father as the kind of man known for kicking the packings out of a guy's ass, and she thought that Morris had run out of fear. Ike didn't buy that, though. Morris just didn't want to do right by Ike's mother. He was probably the kind of guy who liked to make messes everywhere he went. Ike had not ruled out that he probably had a half-brother or sister somewhere out there.

Shortly after pulling in to Oak Bluff, he navigated the neighborhood streets to find McWilliams Mortuary, which sat across from two churches and diagonal to a preschool. The wake would be held the next day, and the funeral would be the day after.

Sitting in the rental car, drumming his fingers against the steering wheel, he realized that somewhere in that structure was the man who had fathered him. An eerie feeling settled over him as he realized that this was the first time he would ever see the old man's face. Instantly his stomach began to bubble with anxiety.

He cranked up the car and continued on down the street to the main strip that intersected the street he was on. He needed a drink. He wasn't much for alcohol, but he couldn't think of anything else that could potentially calm his nerves.

He searched his GPS for a restaurant in the area and found himself circling around downtown until he had come to a dead-end alley, an old train depot on one side, a decrepit brick building on the other. The sign above the front door to the building read "Mack's Shack," and while the place looked to be about to fall in on itself, he figured that if it were open, then it would have a drink stiff enough to help him settle his thoughts.

The inside of the building didn't look much better than the outside. A bubbly redheaded girl escorted him to a table near the middle of the room, and he took a seat in one of the creaky old wooden chairs, feeling its wood strain beneath his two hundred pound frame. He didn't consider himself a heavy man at six foot two, but the chair legs shifting in unison, causing the legs to slant in one direction and then the other—never quite giving out—made him consider whether it was time for a diet. He thought of asking for another chair, but the problem was that all of the chairs looked just as raggedy. A skinny college-age white boy dressed in cargo shorts, flip-flops, and a fitted ringer t-shirt rocked back and forth in his chair, just across from Ike, confident in the fact that the moaning wood would not give out from beneath him. Ike couldn't say that he felt the same. He could, however, keep from tempting the wood by sitting his ass as still as possible while he had his drinks.

After ordering a glass of Jack Daniels, he noticed that there was a band setting up on an elevated stage in the back of the restaurant. Between the drinks and the music, he figured he could buy himself some time to clear his head.

He had no idea of what time McWilliams Mortuary closed, but he had resigned himself to the fact that he would have to just wait until the next day. The traveling and the weirdness of it all were a lot to handle in one day, so he was content to have another glass or two, listen to a few tunes, and check into his hotel to crash for the evening.

The Jack Daniels stung in his chest, and he grimaced. By now a heavyset balding white man with his hair pulled into a ponytail was standing at the microphone in the back, his small band situated behind him. The drummer and guitarist were both white, and the only splash of color on the stage was an elderly black man who sat in a chair with a harmonica resting on his lap.

"Hi, everyone. I'm Ed Wagner. As many of you know, we lost a legend recently, one of the last pure bluesmen from this area, Mr. Morris 'Mojo' Jones."

Ike lifted his head from his glass and nearly fell back out of his chair.

"I know that a lot of folks out there don't even know who this man was," Ed continued, "but you probably know his music when you hear British rock bands like The Crazy Tonies."

Ike's full attention was now focused at the back of the room as he looked at the crowd in front of the stage nodding at each of Ed Wagner's words.

"Yeah," Ed said. "He was a good man—and a good musician. So tonight, we're going to play a few of his songs."

With that, the elderly black man lifted his harmonica and signaled the band to start by dropping his free hand. The music quickly rose, filling the entire room, and when Ed began to sing, his voice imitating a guttural growl, Ike beckoned the waitress and asked for another glass of Jack Daniels.

He watched with consternation how the people in the restaurant nodded attentively to the music, as if they actually enjoyed this imitation of black singing. But while he continued listening, he suddenly became aware of the fact that his own foot was tapping rhythmically beneath the table. He was no fan of the music and didn't want to know anything more about it than what he had to, but now he could sense that the music was doing something to him—to all of them. It was bringing them together (black, white, young, old), and he had to reluctantly admit that there was indeed some kind of power in his father's music. For a moment he wanted to feel that connection, to be a son who knew and had a relationship with his father. He didn't know if it was the alcohol talking, but he almost stood from the table to tell everyone that he was Morris Jones's son. Almost.

Instead, he placed three ten-dollar bills beneath his glass and walked outside. He had a lot to digest before he went by the mortuary the next day, and at that moment all he wanted to do was go to the hotel and call his wife to let her know that, after the first day, he was still standing.

CHAPTER 30

As Ike lay between the cool sheets of his king-sized bed, he tossed and turned, struggling to get his mind to stop racing. It had only been a day, but he missed his girls. He couldn't remember a night where he had not tucked in Rachelle or snuggled up next to Diane, feeling the warmth of her back against his chest. That was one of the main reasons he enjoyed being self-employed: it kept him close to his family.

He even thought about Princess, tail wagging, as she would lick at his fingertips whenever he softly scratched the hair beneath her chin. Damn, he missed her. He could already tell that he would look into getting another dog when he returned home—but he knew he would never be able to replace Princess.

He turned on the lamp next to his bed and opened the wallet lying on the nightstand. He thumbed through pictures of his family. He wanted to hear their voices again, but the clock on his dresser showed that it was two-thirty in the morning. He turned off the light and settled back into bed.

He hadn't expected the people at Mack's Shack to know much about his father—or to respond to his music in the way that they did—and suddenly he was filled with so many questions. There were nearly forty years that his father had had to create some kind of bond. What in the world could the man have been doing to where he couldn't have lifted a finger to at least say "hello"? That was nearly forty birthdays, three graduations, a wedding, and the birth of a granddaughter. Who the hell could turn his back on all of that? Apparently the same man who had written the songs he had heard earlier that evening.

Just the idea of his father being able to blossom as a blues singer stung. The old man had picked the music over him, and Ike didn't know if he could forgive him for that. Still, in a strange way, one that made him confused and upset, he felt a sense of pride when the band had begun playing the music.

He closed his eyes tightly and tried to release each of his thoughts like helium balloons into the night sky. He needed sleep. The next day would be painful enough, and being sleep-deprived would only make matters worse.

He began counting backward from one hundred, his version of counting sheep, and thankfully by the time he had reached thirty-five, he had already drifted off.

When Ike opened his eyes, the sun was beaming through the window of the room. He sat up, wiping the sleep from his eyes, and glanced at the clock on the nightstand. It was 9:30, and while he was still groggy, he forced himself out of bed and into the bathroom to get ready to face the day.

When he stepped outside the hotel, he was struck by how differently Oak Bluff looked from Parsippany. He was used to everything being four lanes, with u-turns that required you to exit and curve around into a perpendicular streetlight to head back in the opposite direction. That had become his frame of reference. Now he was in a town so small, everything was two-lane and narrow, the widest of the streets being Main Street, a street that ran perpendicular to the street on which his hotel was located.

Main Street was the first street he decided to explore. As he navigated the streets, he was surprised at how many of the buildings were actually dilapidated, and it seemed that many of the buildings in the black neighborhoods had suffered even more severe neglect over the years. Then he saw the sign. It was small and simple, but plain as day. The sign read "Blues Museum" and had an arrow signaling to continue driving straight. He followed the sign and made the left turn at the sign several blocks down. He immediately recognized the street, because he could see Mack's Shack near the end of the dead-end, off to his right. He knew that Mack's was not a museum, so he parked his rental car in the parking lot off to the left. That's when he saw the sign in front of the train depot. He had found it.

When he opened the door, he realized that he had entered directly into the gift shop. He walked around, taking in the scene.

"How's it going?"

Ike looked up quickly and saw the guy who had been singing at Mack's the previous night.

"Ed, right?" Ike said.

"How'd you know?" Ed said, his smile signaling that he was happy to be recognized by anyone he did not already know.

"I was at Mack's last night."

"Oh man," Ed said, blushing. "I was trying, but no one could do those songs the way ole Mojo did 'em."

"You did all right," Ike said, nodding to him with a smile.

"Thanks," Ed said, relieved. "I didn't catch your name."

"Oh, my name is Ike."

"Good to meet you, Ike. You visiting Oak Bluff."

"I'm actually here on business, and I, uh, saw this building and just wanted to check it out."

Ed smiled. "Well, welcome to Oak Bluff and to the Blues Museum."

"Thank you." Ike took a look at the souvenirs in the casing beneath his hands. "Do you have anything in here about Morris Jones?"

"Not as much as we should. We have a photograph back there. That's pretty much it. We would love to have more, but he was a private kind of guy, so we didn't really get a chance to develop the kind of relationship with him that we would have liked."

"Can I see the picture?"

"Well," Ed said sheepishly, "it's actually a part of the museum, so there's an admission price."

"How much?"

"Ten."

"Ten dollars to see a picture?"

"Well, there's more than just that picture back there."

Ike smiled. "Fair enough."

He handed Ed ten dollars, and Ed gave him a ticket. Ike glanced at the ticket and thought to himself, "I'm the only one in here. Is a ticket really necessary?"

"Could you point me in the direction of the picture?" Ike asked.

"No problem."

Ed came out from behind the counter and walked through the doorway into the museum, crossing the room to the wall on the right. He stopped at a photograph of a dark complexioned man wearing overalls.

"Here it is."

Ike stared for a moment, considering the face. He could see that he had ears like the old man, but he couldn't see much else that reminded him of himself.

"You a fan?" Ed asked.

"Not really."

"Just curious or something?"

"You could say that."

Ed looked at the picture and looked at Ike. "I hope I don't offend you when I say this—'cause I don't mean it in a bad way at all—but you actually look a little bit like him."

"Think so?" Ike replied.

"Uh, yeah. A little, you know. The ears and the eyes."

"Well, we should," Ike said, turning to face Ed. "He was my father."

CHAPTER 31

When Ike pulled up to McWilliams Mortuary, he steeled himself and got out of the car. He walked slowly toward the front of the building and opened the door. He was quickly greeted by a young man who looked as if he were barely out of high school.

"May I help you?"

"Yeah, I'm here to see Julius McWilliams. I'm Isaiah Jones."

"Oh," the man offered. "I'm very sorry about your loss."

"Yeah, well, thanks."

"I'll go get Mr. McWilliams for you."

As the young man walked away down the corridor, Ike glanced in the room off to his right. It looked like a miniature chapel with rows of chairs lining the room. From his angle, he could only see the chairs positioned to face forward. Slowly, he stepped closer and entered the doorway looking to his right. Everything was angled toward the podium in the slightly elevated pulpit area. The spacing between the chairs and the pulpit was enough to fit a casket. This was where they would have his father's wake.

"Mr. Jones," a voice called to him.

Ike turned to face a very polished man dressed in a dark suit. The salt and pepper beard on the man's face made him look much older than the smoothness of his skin suggested.

"Mr. McWilliams?"

"Good to meet you, although I apologize for the circumstances."

Ike nodded. "Is there anything that I need to do, you know?"

"As I mentioned on the phone, Miss Townsend has taken care of all of the arrangements, including the headstone and cemetery plot."

"Okay."

Ike stood there for a moment, awkward in his silence. Finally, Julius said, "Would you like to see your father?"

"He's ready?" It was a strange question, he knew.

"Sure."

"It's, uh," Ike paused. "You know." He paused again. "I, uh." He stopped, considering his words.

"I understand, Mr. Jones," Julius offered.

"I'm really not sure you do," Ike said.

Julius stood patiently, hands crossed formally in front of him. His poise suggested that little could rattle him.

"You see," Ike started again. "I don't know the man that you guys are about to bury. A few minutes ago, I was at The Blues Museum, and I saw a picture of him on the wall. That was the first time I had ever laid eyes on him. And now," he paused, shaking his head and steadying his voice, "you're telling me that I can *see* my father."

He hadn't expected the emotions to bubble out of him. He could feel the heaviness of water beginning to fill his eyes, but he pressed at his eyelids to stop them in their tracks. He could not bring himself to cry in front of this man.

Julius placed his hand on Ike's shoulder and nodded his understanding.

Ike flinched at Julius's touch. He just wanted to pretend that none of this was happening.

"Whenever you're ready, just walk two doors down on your left. That's our preparation room. We'll have someone open the casket if you want to view the body."

Ike found that he could not even muster the energy to open his mouth. He simply nodded.

Julius walked away to the end of the hall and made a right into what Ike assumed was his office.

Left alone in the hall, Ike considered leaving again. He didn't want a drink though. He wanted out. He wanted to return to Parsippany and forget that he had ever made the trip to Oak Bluff, but his feet began to propel him forward toward the room that housed his father's casket. Before he knew it, he was standing in the doorway looking at a casket in the center of the room. The silence was haunting, but he felt drawn to the casket, as if the polished metal pallbearer bar around it were magnetic.

"Would you like me to open it?" a voice behind him said.

He jumped.

"Yeah, sure."

He stood back as the young man who had greeted him earlier at the door prepared the casket to be opened. When the young man lifted the lid, Ike's eyes locked on the body. Up until that moment, he had no idea of how he would feel when he saw his father. He had built the idea up in his mind that when he finally laid eyes on Morris Jones, a sense of peace would come over him. But looking at the body, he realized that he felt nothing. This was the man who had sired him, yet he could have been anyone, anyone but the man who had caused him to hate his name growing up. As the young man left, Ike realized that it was just he and his father, for the first time, alone together.

He looked at the old man's face, eyes sealed tightly, as if he were a life-sized doll. He had considered ranting his frustrations at the body, but he couldn't bring himself to do it. Instead, he pulled up a folded chair leaning against the wall and sat down.

For some reason, he found himself thinking about the second grade. He didn't even realize that his memory could go back that far. It was something he had not thought about in several decades, yet it materialized in his mind as he looked at his father's body. It was the day that he realized what it meant to not have a father.

His teacher Mrs. Nelson had all of the fathers to come speak to the class one afternoon about what they did for a living. There were police officers, ministers, sanitation workers, plumbers, and even one college basketball coach. The only students who didn't have fathers come in were Roy Evers, whose father was in prison; Daniel Richards, whose father had died in the war; and Ike Jones, whose father's whereabouts were unknown to him or his mother. The other students had picked on him when they learned that he didn't have a father. With Roy, the kids feared his father would bust out of jail and come to get them if they made fun of him. The kids also laid off on Daniel, because his father had sacrificed his life for his country. Ike's father had done neither—as far as he knew—and the kids mocked him for the rest of the year because of it.

By the time he made it to middle school, he realized that a lot of the kids in his class had similar situations, fathers gone AWOL, and it was no longer a big deal. Some of them used it as an excuse to steal, cut classes, and even rob other people. Ike's mother wouldn't have that of her son, though. She clamped down on him so hard some times that he wanted to run away to Mississippi to find his father. At night he would pray for his father to come rescue him from his mother's strictness, but the old man never came. The strictness came in handy, though, when his grades ranked him in the top three graduates of his class. That assured him a scholarship, which was a godsend, since his mother could not afford to send him to college with the money she was making from cleaning houses. Life had been rough for him growing up, and as he looked at his father, he wondered just how much of that would have been different if he had decided to show up.

Then there was the time when Rachelle was born, and all he wanted to do was connect with his father. He had already lost his mother to breast cancer, and the longing to be near one of his own parents was very strong during that first year with the baby. He was willing to forgive everything else if they could just start over.

Most of the time he hated his father—everything about him. He had even considered changing his name to his mother's, but she wouldn't let him while she was alive. Sometimes that made him hate her, too. But he couldn't hate her for long. She was the woman who made sure that he was fed and clothed, the woman who taught him about the birds and the bees, the woman who forced him to get his school work done before he went outside, the woman who whipped his ass to keep him from gang banging, and the woman who made sure that every Christmas she had something under the tree for him.

Morris Jones had missed all of that. Everything. And all Ike wanted to know was *why*.

He looked over the body slowly, hoping to find something in the man's face, his hair, his wrinkled hands, something that could answer that question. He stared, unable to muster up the anger he so badly wanted to expel onto the man. It was just a body, he knew, but Ike had envisioned projecting forty years of anger onto it anyway. Now, he felt only tired. He was tired of hating this man lying before him and tired of blaming him for everything that was not perfect in his life. He was not, however, ready to forgive him. He didn't even know if that was possible.

Ike rose and placed his chair back against the wall. He walked back to the front of the building and told the young man that he would be back later in the evening for the wake.

With that, he walked out into the bright morning sun, sat down in his car, and lowered his head against the steering wheel, crying harder than he ever had in his life.

CHAPTER 32

After picking up a sandwich and a soda, he headed back to his room and slept. He fell into the kind of deep sleep one has after a good cry. And when he awoke, he took a shower and began dressing for the wake.

He could still feel the half-eaten tuna salad sandwich in his stomach and was grateful that he didn't have an appetite. As he stood before the mirror to put on his tie, he thought about the dark brown tie on his own father and how it complemented the old man's simple brown suit. Ike tugged at the lapels of his navy blue suit jacket. He was as ready as he would ever be.

Walking out to the car, he took out his phone and called Diane. He didn't know if he would catch her on an early Friday evening, so he wasn't surprised when he got her voice mail.

"Hey, baby. I'm heading over to the wake now. I'll call you later on this evening. I love you, and give my love to Rachelle."

He slid the phone into his pocket and stood for a moment by the car looking at the auburn and golden hue of the setting sun. He inhaled the air, feeling its cooling breeze brush across his face. The heat rested right beneath the breeze, he surmised, but the breeze felt nice, comforting even.

Ike drove the short distance to the funeral home, collected his thoughts, and walked inside. A handful of people had already assembled in the room holding the wake. He walked in and took a seat near the back. From where he sat, he could see six people scattered throughout the chairs, all of them facing the open casket. Occasionally one of them would walk up to the casket and look into it with sadness and curiosity, staring at the old man's body before returning to his or her seat. Organ music played on a recorded loop in the background. He couldn't stand the hollow sound of a gospel organ. It always reminded him of death, and sitting in the chapel at McWilliams Mortuary was no different. In fact, the music underscored the fact that he was sitting at a wake.

After several minutes of sitting quietly looking toward the front of the room, he noticed, out the corner of his eye, a beautiful young woman looking at him from one of the chairs in the middle of the room. Did she know him? Her attention to him was so bizarre he nearly lifted his left hand so that she could see he was a married man. If that was what she was looking for, she had picked the wrong person and definitely the wrong place.

She stood from her seat and walked back toward him. He could now see the curiosity in her eyes, and he immediately knew who she was.

"Isaiah?" she asked tentatively.

"Erica?" he responded.

She reached out to hug him, and while he embraced her, he had no idea who she was and why she had chosen to pay for the burial of his father.

"I'm so glad that you could come," she said.

"Well, you know. I had to."

"I understand," she said, taking a seat next to him. "I'm sure you have a lot of questions."

"You don't know the half of it."

"If you have a minute, we can step out front."

"Okay."

He stood and followed her outside of the building.

"I've been looking after your father for the last few years," she started.

"Are you a nurse?"

"No. I'm a criminal justice grad student over at Delta State."

"When you say looking after him, what do you mean?" he asked, curious.

"Well, he and my mother dated for about fifteen years, and he took care of her while she was sick, so when she died, I just decided to look in on him to make sure he was doing all right. He was taking pills for his high blood pressure, and he was doing pretty well. He wasn't complaining about anything. So when he died in his sleep, it surprised me, you know?"

Ike nodded. "Did he have any family around here?"

"No one."

Her response helped to confirm that he was not staring into the face of his own sister and not knowing it. She was surely older than fifteen by at least ten years. Her youth, however, made him curious as to how she was able to finance the funeral, which, by all accounts, didn't look like a minor financial expenditure. He thought it would be distasteful to ask flat-out, so he offered to reimburse her for the expenses of the wake and funeral.

"No thank you," she said.

He started to ask her if she was sure, but the look in her eyes said that she had taken control of the situation and that was all there was to it.

The sky darkening around them, he had a million questions he wanted to ask, and at the same time he had no questions at all.

"You're the reason Julius called me, aren't you?" he finally asked.

"Yeah."

"So you knew about me? He told you he had a son?"

She nodded.

"So he could tell *you*, but he couldn't reach out to me on his own?" He could feel the pain from earlier bubbling to the surface again.

"It was complicated," she started. "Before I say any more, I think that he would have wanted to let you know that he loved you."

"Pardon me if I find that to be a crock of shit."

She lowered her head for a moment as if looking for a new approach. She looked at him and said, "He had actually wanted to be a part of your life, but it didn't work out that way."

"Well, this is all news to me."

"But it probably isn't news to your mother."

"Hold on," he said, backing away from her. "You don't know my mother, God rest her soul, so don't even bring her into this. That woman raised me all by herself. I know you're not about to stand there and blame my mother for all of this."

"I'm not blaming anyone for anything."

She stopped for a moment to give him a chance to cool off.

"Isaiah, there are two things that can happen here. You can let me tell you what I know from what your father actually said to me, or you can tell me that none of it matters, and I can let you go about your business without having to hear any of this."

Ike looked at the street that ran in front of the funeral home. He knew she was right. This was the moment he wondered would ever happen: learning the truth about his father. One part of him wanted to hear every last detail that she could provide; the other side felt no obligation to hearing any of his father's words. But wasn't that what his trip had been about—on some level? He had come to learn something, possibly the truth, about his father, and what Erica was telling him now was that he would have to put his pride aside if he wanted real answers.

Although he could feel his temples beginning to throb with the hint of a migraine, he returned his gaze to Erica.

"Tell me."

Erica nodded and opened her mouth slowly. "Did your mother ever tell you how you came to be in Chicago?"

"She said that she had left a bad relationship and needed a change of environment."

"Well, there's a little bit more to the story. When your mother got pregnant with you, her father came looking for Mojo. In those days, if a woman got pregnant, the man had to marry her so the child would be legitimate. So her father came to talk about a shotgun wedding."

"A shotgun wedding?" Ike asked.

"Yeah, it was a quick wedding that was done for one reason only: to keep the kid from being legally recognized as a bastard. It didn't matter if the man and woman got a divorce one week later. The kid had to be right with the law."

"So my father must have split then."

Erica swallowed and paced her voice. "He was a kid, Isaiah. He was scared. See, he actually spent a lot of his teenage years working on a sheriff's ranch—a kind of juvenile detention center —where he did what he had to do to survive. His parents and brothers had already died, so he had been in survival mode for a while. When your grandfather came looking for him, he panicked. After that, your grandfather sent your mother to live in Chicago, because the community frowned on unwed mothers."

"Umh," Ike grunted to himself as he considered all of this. Why was he just now hearing this story? He wondered what else Erica was about to tell him that would alter his understanding of everything that he had believed to be true about his family.

"So you were born in Chicago," she said, continuing, "and that's about all that Mojo knew for sure. It took him a while to get an address for you and your mother because no one wanted to help him after he had brought such shame to your mother's family. Then when you were about three or so, he had managed to get an address from someone, and he immediately reached out to your mother. As you can imagine, she still had hurt feelings about everything that had happened, so she sent him a letter that basically told him to go to hell. He continued to write to her and plead to see you, but none of the other letters got answered. So the trail went cold for a while.

"A few years later he managed to get hold of a phone number, and he started calling to Chicago. By this time your mother was in a relationship and didn't want anything to do with him. She refused to take any more calls from him, so he started mailing money to the address he had. He never heard back from her."

"I see," Ike said.

He didn't know how to feel about any of this. Erica was essentially telling him that he had been a pawn in a larger game between two people battling with their own pride issues.

"After fifteen years of going back and forth with your mother, you all moved and he could never find you again."

Ike sighed. "You know, it's easy to sit here and see it all as him being the victim because he couldn't get to me, but as a father, I know for a fact that there is nothing that would keep me from my daughter."

"I understand," Erica said. "I don't want to make any excuses for Mojo. He might not have gone about this the right way, but he did it the only way he knew how. It was only after he passed that I was able to comb through everything he had in the house and get on the Internet to try to find you. It took a minute, but I was able to track you to your last job and then your new company website. I could tell by the picture it was you, so I told Mr. McWilliams how to contact you."

Ike nodded, impressed at what one could accomplish through the Internet these days.

"Let me tell you a story," he said. "When I graduated from high school, I put together an invitation for him. Put his name on the outside of the envelope and everything. All I had was his name. Deep down I was hoping that my graduation would be the event that would bring him to Chicago. He would know that his son was doing well, moving forward, you know? When I went to my mother to see if she could help me get an address, she told me that she didn't have anyway of knowing how to contact him. I almost mailed the invitation with just his name and the word 'Mississippi' written beneath it. Mama said that it would never make it to him though, not with so much information missing. And you want to hear something funny? I still have that invitation. I couldn't mail it, but I still kept it."

He could feel his eyes begin to water, and he looked away.

"I guess I always thought he'd find me. That was the child in me, looking for a father. Then I grew up."

Erica nodded, her arms crossed to shield herself from the cooling air. "I know this is all too little and too late, but Mojo viewed not getting to know you as his biggest regret."

"Well, that's interesting," Ike responded, brushing a tear from his cheek. "You know, because of him, I am a good father and husband. I am everything that he couldn't be to me and my mother."

"I'm sure he would be happy for you."

"Yeah, well. I don't know how much real credit he could've taken, since he missed out on every single important event in my life."

"I feel where you're coming from," she said. "It's a messed up situation—and I'm not saying that it's not messed up—but it has to mean something to have the other side of the story now."

"It does, Erica. It does. But it's going to take me a while to figure out what that something is supposed to be."

CHAPTER 33

THE FUNERAL

In the early, early hours of morning, a soft rain swept across the streets of Oak Bluff. The gentleness of it all went undetected by nearly everyone sleeping through the night. In fact, by the time the sun rose, the water had all but disappeared, as if it had never occurred.

The brightness of the sun touched Ike as he lay on his back looking at the ceiling of his hotel room. Today was the day.

Everything that Erica had told him was still swirling around his brain, and it all left a funny taste in his mouth. He hated that she had managed to cast some level of suspicion on his mother's motives for shielding him from his father. That idea alone continued to gnaw at him. There was absolutely no way of being able to confirm any of these things, mainly because all of the principal parties were no longer around to talk to.

The funeral was set to begin at eleven that morning, so he began to get cleaned up. As he dressed, the familiarity of having done the same thing the previous day crept over him. He was in a loop like a scratched record skipping over and over. He would be happy to break the loop and return to Parsippany when the day was over.

He had agreed to meet Erica at the McWilliams Mortuary to ride over to the funeral in the limousine she had gotten to transport the family members and close friends. Apparently the funeral was to be held at the cemetery, per the wishes of Mojo, and unless Ike had spent time in Oak Bluff moving about in the county, he might have trouble finding it on his own.

When he pulled up to the funeral home, he noticed that Erica was already there on the side of the building talking to a young man. She seemed a bit upset, but the young man seemed to be trying to reassure her, comfort her. Ike rolled down the window of his car and waved at her. He could see her excuse herself from the young man and walk toward the car.

"You all right?" Ike asked.

"Yes. I'm okay," she responded, clearly ruffled by the episode that had just taken place.

"If you need me to speak to that young man over there, I will," he offered.

"No, that's okay. I can handle him. How are you doing, though?"

He smiled. "You know. It is what it is."

"I feel you."

For a moment they looked silently in different directions.

"We should be pulling out of here in the next half hour, so you might want to grab a quick bite to eat before we leave."

"I don't really have much of an appetite."

"I understand. It's just that we have a little ride ahead of us, and I didn't want you to get hungry."

"Well, maybe I should get a cup of coffee or something—just in case."

"That probably wouldn't be a bad idea," she said, smiling.

"All right. Well, I'll be back in a few minutes."

As he pulled away from the parking lot, he noticed Erica walking back over to the young man in his rearview mirror, and he immediately understood the expression on her face: it wasn't so much frustration, as it was that she really cared for the young man.

THE RIDE TO THE CEMETERY WAS QUIET AS THE TWO OF them sat opposite each other in vehicle far too large for two people. When he looked at Erica, he could tell that her mind was elsewhere, which he didn't mind. His thoughts drifted back and forth between everything that had happened over the past week. He remembered that somber drive to the vet with Princess. He remembered the last time he made love to his wife. He remembered Rachelle waving goodbye at the airport. He remembered what it was like pulling into Memphis International and driving to Oak Bluff. He remembered Mack's Shack and The Blues Museum and what it felt like the moment he heard his father's music and saw his picture. His was so lost in his thoughts that it took him a moment to realize that Erica was talking to him.

"Isaiah! Over there. That's where your father lived."

He looked at the simple house just off of the thin country road.

About a quarter of a mile down, the limo turned and headed toward a green tarp near the back of a small cemetery. There were already cars parked off to the side and some people already assembled beneath the tarp.

The hearse was parked ahead of them, but he could see the casket was already elevated above the gravesite, a green blanket covering the earthy mound that spread out from the plot. An usher escorted Erica and him to two reserved seats that sat at the front of the tent-like structure. With the actual grave off to the right, a small podium had been centered in front of the chairs, and a balding older man in a black suit with a large crucifix hanging from his collar asked everyone to settle down so the program could begin.

"Today we have come together to say goodbye to a good man, Mr. Morris Jones. He, ahh, wasn't a man of a lot of words. He chose, ahh, to talk with his instrument."

In the back of the tent someone giggled softly, and Ike scrunched up his face. He was already wondering why the pastor was in full "preacher" mode so early in the service, but the chuckle had distracted him and made him realize that the word "instrument" might have had more than one meaning.

"We know, ahh, that Mr. Jones didn't spend a lot of time in church, ahh, but, ahh, we know he had his own relationship with the Lord, and, ahh, that's all that matters."

Ike sighed. This man didn't appear to know much about his father, other than the fact that his father wasn't a regular church-goer. He just hoped that this wasn't the man who would be eulogizing him.

The pastor read a lengthy scripture, but Ike's mind drifted as he stared at the casket. When he saw Erica stand up, he almost stood himself, thinking that they were supposed to stand together.

She took her place behind the podium, and for the first time, Ike actually focused on who was speaking.

"My name is Erica Townsend, and most of you know that Mojo and my mother were together for fifteen years. I can't really speak too much about what happened before he met my mother, but I can tell you a lot about what he was like from then forward.

"He was a kind man, a loving man, a man who would've given you his last. When my mother got sick, he could've run, but he didn't. He stayed, and he helped me to get through one of the most difficult times of my life."

Erica wiped her eyes, and one of the ushers standing off to the side placed a hand on her shoulder for comfort. "He was a simple man, and he was a talented man. He wasn't perfect, though. Not by a long shot. He did a lot of things that he regretted, but he tried his best to leave everything a little better than he found it."

Ike swallowed hard as he met her gaze.

"He didn't want a regular eulogy for his funeral," she said. "No offense, Pastor James, but he didn't want someone who didn't really know him to talk about him over his body. He always said that it's hard to talk about someone that you didn't really know." She looked over at the casket. "Mojo, I hope you don't mind that I asked Pastor James to give a little scripture for you. It was out of love," she said, smiling.

Erica turned to face the crowd again. "If anyone has anything that they'd like to share about how Mojo might have touched them, please come forward and share a few words."

Ike watched as Ed Wagner, the only white man present, took his place at the podium.

"I'm Ed Wagner, and I run The Blues Museum. I just wanted to say that Morris "Mojo" Jones was a pioneer, an artist of the first order. He was able to learn, not only to play an instrument, but also write music, and express the joys and pains of millions of people, just through the sound of his voice and strings of his guitar. And he did all of this without formal training. He inspired people locally, nationally, and internationally. He was a legend, and his contributions to the arts will never be forgotten. Thank you."

Ed left the podium and walked over to Ike, extending his hand in condolence, before hugging Erica and returning to his seat.

The next person to walk to the podium was the young man Ike had seen earlier that morning at the funeral home.

"Good morning, everyone," the young man began. "My name is Coltrane Washington, and I first came here to Oak Bluff nearly two weeks ago to write an article on Mr. Jones for a magazine called *Midnight Jukebox*."

Ike opened his eyes in surprise. He knew the name Coltrane

Washington because he had bought *The Wine of Goddesses* for Diane last year as a Mother's Day gift. He hadn't expected anyone famous to be speaking at his father's funeral. And Coltrane looked much younger than Ike had expected him to be, which was at least his own age, especially to have written a book like that. He refocused his thoughts as he continued to listen.

"I had come here with this article on Mojo that I just submitted to my editor," Coltrane said, lifting a few sheets of paper from the podium, "but being here and seeing all of you, I just want to speak from the heart. I just want to tell you what I experienced from this man, and I don't need these pages to do that." Placing the pages in the inner pocket of his black suit coat, he continued, "I have to admit that I didn't know anything about Mojo before I came here. I wasn't what you'd call the most qualified person to be writing an article on a blues legend, but I decided to take a chance, the same way that Mojo decided to take a chance as a bluesman at a time when his options were to pick several hundred pounds of cotton by nightfall or leave for The North to get a job in some factory. He created a path for himself that did not exist. And along the way, he created some of the most memorable blues music ever. He touched a lot of hearts. Yeah, he was definitely a one-of-a-kind man. But the thing that impressed me most about him was that he did all of this while maintaining a humility that betrayed his personal successes. He wasn't arrogant or distant. He struck me as the kind of man who would talk to anyone who happened to find his way onto his porch. He also taught me how it was okay to open yourself up to all of the possibilities of life, and for that, I can honestly say that I am a better man for having known him."

Coltrane walked toward Ike and, following suit, shook his hand, but when he reached Erica, he knelt down beside her chair, and she embraced him warmly, kissing him gently on his lips. Coltrane stood, slowly pulling his fingers away from Erica's hand as he returned to his seat near the rear of the tent.

When Ike returned his eyes toward the front of the tent, he noticed that Pastor James had returned.

"Is there anyone else who would like to share something this morning?"

In the quiet shuffling of chairs and quiet mumblings, the wail of a high-pitched voice cut through the air. Ike quickly turned to face Erica to see if she had broken down. As the second pitch came, he realized that what he was hearing was not a woman's voice, but the sound of a guitar. Walking around the side of the tent was a teenaged boy. The boy walked up and stood next to the podium, an old, worn guitar in hand. The boy began to play a song that sounded eerily like one that he had had heard two nights earlier at Mack's Shack. The kid's eyes were closed, as he played each note to perfection, the strings vibrating above the sound hole, his fingers tickling the strings intimately.

While the boy's hand moved up and down the fret board, Ike found himself smiling. With each note of the guitar, it was as if his father were talking to him. With the sun high in the sky, the flat green land extending on for miles behind him, the boy appeared to almost channel Mojo.

Ike smiled and closed his eyes. He could feel something deep within him beginning to let go, something telling him that it was time to forgive.

When the boy finished, amid applause, he removed the guitar strap from his shoulder and walked over to the casket, gingerly placing the guitar on top of the closed casket, careful to balance it so that it did not fall. Having done so, he walked out the side of the tent and continued walking out into the morning countryside.

Ike leaned over and whispered to Erica, "Who was that? He was amazing!"

"I believe his name is Jason. He was a friend of your father's," she whispered in response.

Pastor James returned to the podium. "Are there any others?"

Hearing no response, he continued. "Well, Miss Townsend, if you don't mind, I'll give the benediction now."

Ike smiled as he listened to the pastor's voice, his spirit lightening. There were still many questions—with no way of ever getting the answers—but that didn't bother him as much as he thought it would.

He knew he would soon be returning home to his wife and daughter, and when the time was right, he would tell them what he knew of his father, the bluesman.

SOUNDTRACK

1. "Rattle Snake Blues" by Charley Patton

No Delta blues list would be complete without the father of the blues, Charley Patton, a man whose playing not only inspired other blues musicians, but gave rise to the genre as a whole.

2. "Crossroad Blues" by Robert Johnson

Behind the mythology of Robert Johnson and alleged deal with the devil lies a musician, who, outside of Charley Patton, is one of the most regarded and widely recognized of Delta bluesmen.

3. "Smokestack Lightnin'" by Howlin' Wolf (Side note: he is from my hometown of West Point, Mississippi (in the White Station section)

Howlin' Wolf would have been one of the bluesmen that Morris "Mojo" Jones most admired. Howlin' Wolf's style of music and his onstage antics (licking his guitar, etc.) were techniques that Mojo would emulate in his own shows. This is referenced in the scene where Ed Wagner describes to Coltrane Washington his experience of seeing Mojo live at a juke joint.

4. "Got My Mojo Working" by Muddy Waters

Muddy Waters is another artist Mojo would have emulated, more in terms of musical style. Like Mojo, Muddy Waters's music was covered by English rock bands. In fact, Muddy Water's song "Rolling Stone" is the namesake for the rock group of the same name.

5. "Last Two Dollars" by Johnnie Taylor

This song represents the direction of the evolution of blues music. This is the kind of song Coltrane would have heard on the radio or in a juke joint upon visiting Oak Bluff. These songs might sound like rhythm and blues to the novice listener, but in Mississippi, this is considered blues music.

6. "How Blue Can You Get" by B.B. King

B.B. King has, for over sixty years, served as the unofficial ambassador and face of blues music. He is also considered one of the most successful bluesmen of all time. This song would be the type of song that would have put a big smile on Mojo's face as he sat on the porch of his shotgun house and stared off into the horizon. It is also the kind of song that appeals to those who have more "neo-blues" tastes (like Johnnie Taylor and Tyrone Davis).

7. "Boom Boom" by John Lee Hooker

This song deals with a man being completely taken with a woman. The song aptly illustrates Coltrane's reaction to Erica when he begins to get to know her.

8. "Like Mom's Apple Pie" by Tyrone Davis

This is one of the songs Coltrane heard on the radio on his first trip to Oak Bluff. This is a song that Jason would have known as well, as it would have been on the radio, just like Johnnie Taylor's "Last Two Dollars." The song is more representative of what contemporary blues sound like. It would have also been the type of song played in some of the juke joints that drew older crowds.

9. "Strokin'" by Clarence Carter

This song is unabashedly about sex, one of the favorite topics of a good blues song. I'm still amazed at how much airplay this got in my community when I was growing up. Even with the curse word and the constant references to sex, the song was embraced by young and old alike for its rawness, a staple of good blues music.

10. "Big Fat Mama Blues" by Tommy Johnson

Tommy Johnson is actually the person who made the deal with the devil at the Crossroads, but his legacy is often overshadowed by Robert Johnson's. (While some dispute Robert Johnson made a deal with the devil, few people dispute that Tommy Johnson did.) This song would have been a song that helped to shape Mojo's approach to his blues music.

ALSO BY RAN WALKER

ACKNOWLEDGMENTS

I would like to thank my family (extended and nuclear), as well as the following individuals: The Whittingtons, Sabin Duncan, Kyr Mack, Jewel Bush, Phill Branch, the Son Edna Foundation, the Mississippi Arts Commission, the National Endowment for the Arts, Tyehimba Jess, Van G. Garrett, the Callaloo Writers Workshop, Thomas Glave, Nelly Rosario, Eric Tanyavutti, DaMaris Hill, Nancy Garcia, Aaron Vano, Christi Cartwright, L. Lamar Wilson, Brandi Ray, Dr. John Alewynse, Dr. David Green, Dr. Amee Carmines, Diane Williams, Erica "Rivaflowz" Buddington, Kathryn DeShields, Christopher R. Hardiman, Jay Craft, Nsayel Mputubwele, and Fonzworth Bentley.

I would also like to thank everyone who has ever taught me, inside and outside the classroom. And to those of you who continue to support my writing by reading my books, I thank you from the bottom of my heart.

Last, but by no means least, I'd like to thank my father for never giving up on this book and my wife for never giving up on me.

ABOUT THE AUTHOR

Ran Walker is the author of twenty-one books. He is the winner of the 2019 Indie Author of the Year and 2019 BCALA Fiction Ebook Awards. He teaches creative writing at Hampton University and lives with his wife and daughter in Virginia. Ran can be reached via his website, www.ranwalker.com.